ACKNOWLEDGMENTS

All praise be to God, Lord of my world! Nobody told me that the sky was the limit. So I grew up with a fear of heights, like every one of the men that became my brothers in the streets. I'm not gonna name all of you, just the ones that started from the bottom with me and have always had my back: J. McNutt a.k.a. Flex, M. Danley a.k.a. Moe, D. Ashford a.k.a. Dee, them Cunningham brothers—RIP—Tim and Alfonica "Junior" Jones, J. Ross a.k.a. Daddy O., and D. Wayett a.k.a. Damoe. Like I said, I'm not going to name all of you, and if you know me then you know it's all love with us. I send my love and prayers to my beautiful children and the women who made them. I need to say thank you to my dad for stepping up as much as he could for me in my time of need—RIP, Jim Ray Jones III. I miss you much. I just have to put this name in here because she's crazy and I don't want to hear it LOL: Orean Harper a.k.a. Chocolate, and family. Look, I'll have more room to add everyone else in my next one, because I'm not done yet. Thank You to G2G for taking me in and bringing my dream to life.

SHADES OF

REV

ASSA RAYMOND BAKER

Good2Go Publishing

SHADES OF REVENGE

Written by Assa Ray Baker

Cover Design: Davida Baldwin

Typesetter: Mychea

ISBN: 9781947340183

Copyright ©2018 Good2Go Publishing

Published 2018 by Good2Go Publishing

7311 W. Glass Lane • Laveen, AZ 85339

www.good2gopublishing.com

https://twitter.com/good2gobooks

G2G@good2gopublishing.com

www.facebook.com/good2gopublishing

www.instagram.com/good2gopublishing

SHADES OF REVENGE

Chapter 1

TGIF! Everyone everywhere was rushing to get ready for the weekend. Most carwashes and beauty shops were packed. It seemed like the entire city of Milwaukee was out. Days like this for a true diehard hustler were the best time to move around in the streets.

Jasso drove to Kilwaukee's north side, taking full advantage of the crowded streets that evening. Kilwaukee was the nickname given to the city after a spike in the city's body count. It seemed like gangsters and young thugs were killing throughout its rundown neighborhoods. Jasso fit right in. He knew not to drive too fast or too slow, so he would not draw unwanted attention from the local police, especially with sixty pounds of kush sitting in a box on the backseat.

Jasso was driving a plain, light gray Chevy minivan that he only used to make runs like the one he was doing tonight. Today he was alone, but most of the time he had one of his Latin King brothers with him, especially if he felt a certain way about the neighborhood he was visiting. He pulled his black and gold *M* fitted cap down low to meet the Ray-Ban sunglasses he wore, even though the van's windows were lightly tinted, and the sun was setting for the night. Jasso looked the part of a typical Latino delivery driver on his way to or coming from a call without a care in the world.

~ ~ ~

Asad was parked on the third level of the Grand Mall parking garage. He sat in his rented maroon Ford Five Hundred sipping on a cold cherry iced tea waiting for his weed connect to make it to him and his girlfriend who lived in the lofts over the mall. He thought of running in and buying an outfit to go out in later that night, but he didn't want to have Jasso waiting, even though he was already a few minutes late. So, he picked up his phone and checked his Facebook page. He posted and then accepted and denied a few friend requests over whom he felt his girlfriend wouldn't have a heart attack.

"What it do, FB? A boss trying to get up out there tonight. So, tell me, where's the party at?"

Responses poured in within seconds. Asad traded comments with his followers and wondered if his girlfriend, China, would be ready when he called.

2

She was all of five feet even, and thick in all the right places. China's complexion was the color of honey, and she had long, jet-black hair that few knew about because she loved wearing laced wigs. She would not be seen outside looking like a hot mess at any time of the day, which is why she took so long to get ready whenever it was time to go anywhere. Asad really didn't mind, because he knew she did it to look good for him.

~ ~ ~

Jasso glanced at his iced-out, white-gold Movado watch. He knew that he was late already. Both the road construction on 6th Street and the always crowded downtown city traffic made his drive to drop off work to Asad even longer than any other trip he made. Once he finally made it through the mess of construction, he had to wait for a slow-moving window shopper to walk across the street.

Next, he made a quick right turn, drove through the entrance, and then made another right into the parking garage, where he had to stop and retrieve a parking pass before being allowed to go any further. The barrier arm went slowly up, and he took his foot off the brake and let the van crawl forward as he took out his phone to speed-dial Asad.

"I'm here, homie. Where you at?"

"I'm right here looking at you, bro!" Asad answered, before he flashed his headlights, so Jasso could see him.

"Okay, okay! I see you."

He ended the call as he pulled into the slot next to the Ford.

Asad got out of his car and in with Jasso.

"It's all there," he explained as he handed a bag containing the cash he owed him for the weed.

"I know, bro. That's why I fuck with you the way I do. Your bread is always on point!" he complimented.

Out of habit, he took a quick look inside the envelope before putting the brown paper bag in the door compartment.

"I put a little something extra in for you. It should hold you over until I come back. I gotta go out of town for this wedding."

"Yeah, I remember you telling me the wifey was on you about that awhile back."

"I did? Shit, homie! I be blowed so much, I can't remember shit no more!" Jasso stated while picking up an unfinished blunt from the ashtray. "Anyhow, bro, there's sixty for you back there if you can handle it."

He took a deep pull of the blunt.

"If you can't, let me know now, and I'll set something else up for you with one of the brothas.

4

Maybe King Leo."

"No, I'm good! I got you. You seem to have forgotten how I get money, like the hood is an ATM. I'm good, bro! Plus, I don't wanna fuck with nobody else. The next nigga might not keep it trill like you do, and I don't wanna fuck up what we got."

He climbed into the back of the van to get the big paper box.

"When you think you going to be back, because it's gonna take me longer than a week with this here."

"We going to be gone a little longer than that. My lady's trying to spend time with her sisters and shit."

Jasso shook his head and exhaled the kush smoke.

"But, Ace, man, you need to work on your time. I'm about to flood you with this pack. So, sell 'em whole—whatever. Just get your flip time up. You know my motto: 'Get 'em in and get 'em gone.' It's time to step your game up."

"Say no mo'! I'ma hit you when I'm done," Asad assured Jasso, before he then climbed out of the rear door of the van with the box.

Jasso stayed put until Asad had the box in his car. He then tapped the horn two quick times as he pulled off. He retraced the way he came in, to get out. After paying the parking fee, Jasso made a left turn into traffic, but he was unaware of the white 1995 Chevy Impala pulling out in traffic four cars behind him.

~ ~ ~

Once Jasso's van was out of Asad's sight, he pulled the box back out of the rental where he put it to throw Jasso off. Jasso didn't need to know this was a place where Asad sometimes laid his head at night or that his girlfriend lived here, just in case things ever went south with him and Jasso one of these days.

Asad called China as he made his way across the busy mall floor.

"Bae, I need you to meet me at the elevator right fast. I'm on my way up now."

"Right now, bae? I'm doing my lashes."

"Yeah. What part of right quick didn't you understand? Get your ass up and do what the fuck I said!"

"Boy, stop! You better get you some kids to talk to like that or put a ring on a bitch finger," she responded, knowing he was joking with her.

She finished carefully putting on her first lash.

"Bae, I thought we was going to leave right away after you handle your business. What changed?" China pouted.

It was her only full day off after working all that week, and she was ready to let loose.

"Nothing! I'm done with that. I just gotta do something first, and I need you to go buy me something to wear. I'ma get dressed over here," he explained.

He knew that she loved to shop and keep his clothes at her place. Asad knew China wanted him to move in with her, but he had a bit of an issue with a woman controlling where he laid his head.

"You mean buy *us* something to wear? I know you don't think you gonna buy an outfit to step out in and not me?"

She finished the lashes on her other eye, and then rushed out to meet him at the elevator.

He got another call that he knew was about cash, so he gave in to his girl and answered his other line.

"What up, sis?" he greeted when he answered his other phone.

"What it do, bro-bro. You good yet? I need to put something in the air like right now, 'cause muthafuckas been blowing my phone up. So, tell me we good?" Sky said.

He laughed at the thought of her jonesing for a blunt.

"Yeah, I got you. I'm getting her dressed right now! I'll hit you when I'm outside your spot," he told her, before picking up the box that he had set down to get his other phone out of his pocket.

"Cool, cool! I'll tell 'em I'ma be good in like twenty or thirty minutes?" she said, fishing for a time frame.

7

"Alright, see you about then," he agreed, before he ended the call at the same time the doors opened.

China stood there with a puzzled look on her face.

"Noooo, nigga! Don't get off the phone with the bitch now that I'm here!"

"China, don't start that shit. That was Sky. She's ready for me, and you know how sis gets when she ain't got nothing to smoke. So, stop it!"

He set the box back down and counted out $500 with which she could shop.

"What the fuck ever!"

She snatched a few more bills out of his hand and ran away playfully.

"That's for making me feel this way," she pouted, and then smiled over her shoulder.

"Yeah, yeah! Just please don't be all fucking day, China!" he yelled behind her as the other elevator doors closed.

Asad knew his girl like a good book. China would never give up on a chance to shop. But it would also give him the time he needed to put the weed together for Sky and a few other customers he had waiting on his line.

Asad liked the apartment over the mall; not only because the mall below kept China busy at times like this, but also because it was safe from both police and would-be robbers. In fact, a couple of officers lived on the same floor. The best part was that no one knew he pretty much lived there, and no one ever questioned him when he had them meet him there to make a purchase. He knew he needed to take a chance and move in. Asad really didn't think China was the kind of woman that liked to get mad and put her man out every week, but then he wasn't the type of guy to give her a reason.

After wrestling with a big compressed bale, Asad broke down a Philly and rolled up a fat blunt for himself before he got to work weighing out pounds and ounces.

Chapter 2

Jasso sat at a red light on 16th and National waiting for it to turn green so he could move on. One of Milwaukee's finest pulled up next to him. Out of pure reflex, Jasso put his elbow on the center console and cupped his face with his hand. He was known by most of the south-side police force, which is why he tried to hide as much of his face as he could, not even thinking about the tinted windows of the van. Jasso willed for the light to change or the cop car to pull off. He didn't care which came first. He just wanted to be far away from the cops before they got any bright ideas to pull him over.

The light turned green. The cop made a hard left blaring the car siren as he raced down National. Traffic on 16th street wasn't as slow moving as it was downtown, so the driver in back of Jasso blew his horn, breaking him from his state of shock. He pulled off without looking back to see who it was that blew the horn at him, and he didn't slow down until he came to a stop at the next set of stop lights.

A McDonald's was right across the street, so Jasso decided to get something to eat. He liked to go inside because he had a thing for one of the cashiers, a gorgeous black and Mexican girl with short, curly brown hair.

The Impala pulled in and parked on the far side of the parking lot. The entire time, its passengers never took their eyes off Jasso until he disappeared inside the restaurant.

"We should move on his ass now. Just as soon as he comes out!" Boony suggested as he put the car in park.

"You know I'm with it. I'm hungry anyway," Freebandz seconded from the backseat, after passing on the blunt he was smoking.

"Fuck that! We gonna wait and stay on this nigga until he takes us to his stash house," Eshy informed the others, before he took a deep pull off the blunt. "My trigger finger's telling me the punk is about to take us right there right the fuck now."

Eshy took another pull of the weed and then passed it on.

"Get it all or nothing, fam! I feel you, but I need some cash," Boony agreed as he finished off the weed.

~ ~ ~

Ten minutes later the Impala caught the seasoned thug's eye on his way back to his van. Jasso climbed inside feeling like he had seen it somewhere before, but he then shook it off as paranoia.

"I gotta stop smoking this shit like this!" he joked to himself as he dumped tobacco out of a Swisher Sweet cigar.

After he finished rolling the blunt, Jasso glanced over his shoulder at the car once more before pulling out of the lot. He tried to look in it as he passed, but couldn't make out the faces because of its blacked-out windows. This did nothing for Jasso's paranoia. The wheels screeched as Boony backed out of the parking slot. High off the laced blunt, they missed Jasso getting back into his van; and by the time they saw him, he was almost out of sight. Boony floored it to catch up to him.

Jasso told himself if he was being followed, he was going to make them show themselves. With that thought, he made a sudden turn and then punched it down the street until he came to the stop sign on the next corner. He sat and waited for the car to do the same thing as it tried to catch up with him.

"Fam, did you see him make that left?" Eshy pointed out excitedly.

"I got this. This nigga ain't getting away from me!" Boony announced as he stomped on the accelerator.

The big V8 shot the car forward. But when they hit the corner, they saw the van make a quick right.

"I think he knows we on his ass!"

Jasso saw the car and knew he was no longer just being paranoid. He turned right and then left into the alley as he raced to the other end and made a left onto the street. He raced up the block and turned down another alley, where he quickly pulled into someone's driveway. He got out of the van and peeked around the corner of the back of the house next to which he had parked. In order to get home, Jasso wanted to see if he had lost them or if he would have to shoot it out with whoever was in the car.

The Impala turned where the van turned, but they didn't see it. Boony raced up and down the side streets looking for the van.

"Where in the fuck did he go?" he yelled as he slowed down, so they wouldn't get stopped by the police.

"Shit! You lost him! The nigga can't be that far away. He must have hidden somewhere!" Eshy said angrily. "Hit some of these alleys. He might be hiding in one!"

They spent the next ten minutes or so criss-crossing the streets hoping to find Jasso.

"Fuck! That fag-ass nigga got away!" Boony spat as he turned and headed back to the north side until they got another chance at their mark.

~ ~ ~

Later that night after Asad made a few moves to get things in motion with the weed he had copped earlier, he and China dressed in the outfits that he had sent her to buy and they then hit the city. China wanted to go to All Stars on Fond du Lac, and since Asad had never been there, he didn't mind. Besides, he didn't want to upset her any more than he already had, when he told her the good and bad news about his meetup with Jasso. The good news was that he would be making more money, but the bad news was that he would be away from her more often in order to make it happen.

All Stars was packed, and everyone seemed to be having a good time out on the dance floor. China went straight to the ladies' room, while Asad grabbed them a spot at the bar until she came out. The music was good, and Jasso was soon surrounded by a lot of the city-grown and sexy patrons.

"What can I get for you, handsome?" one of the servers asked, after she dropped off drinks to a guy not far from him.

"Let me get a bottle of Grey Goose, a draft, and a Jolly Rancher with a lemon."

Jasso gave her his and China's orders. She always got the same drink whenever they went out, so he knew it by heart.

When the drinks arrived Asad downed a double shot of Goose right away, before he then sipped on his beer and checked out the Bucks game on the television behind the bar. He saw the Bucks were down by five to the Lakers' seventy-seven points in the fourth quarter.

Jasso looked over toward the ladies' room and wondered what China was doing in there so long. He hoped he would see her walk out, but instead, he locked eyes with a slim red-bone girl coming his way. She had a long golden ponytail that was tipped in red. She was dressed in a tight, short floral dress and was carrying an empty glass in her hand. Asad must have looked too long because the woman took it as an invitation to join him.

"Who's winning?" Slim asked, taking a seat next to him and arching her back so he could get a good look at her big tits.

He thought her lashes were too long and took away from her hazel eyes.

"I think it's seventy-nine to seventy."

Slim leaned in closer so she could be heard over the music.

"Do you like it?"

"Do I like what?" he asked, trying not to look down her low-cut dress.

"The game! Unless you see something else you like?"

"Yeah, it's okay. It looks like the Bucks might win one if they keep playing like they are now," he replied while trying to avoid her flirt.

"It's Summer!" she told him with a smile.

"What?" he asked as he took a drink of his beer.

"My name is Summer."

"Okay, and I'm here with my girl!" Asad told her, not wanting to fall into one of China's games.

He thought Summer was one of her friends from work or someplace trying to help China prove that he was a cheater.

"Okay, so your wifey left you all by yourself? You must be a good one," she asked, still trying to make the catch.

"You can ask her when she gets back—and maybe we can all be friends."

He smiled and started to play a game of his own.

"Is that right?" Summer answered as she put her hand on his. "I don't see no harm in that," she said, just as China walked up.

"Who is this, Asad?" China asked with real attitude in her voice.

"I don't know. You tell me!" he continued to play along.

"I'm Summer, bitch! Ask me if you wanna know something about me, bitch!"

She was so loud that people turned to see what was going on, hoping to see a fight.

Four guys stopped what they were doing and quickly came over to Summer. Asad stood up in front of his girl, shielding her with his six-foot frame and two hundred pounds.

"It's cool! We don't want no trouble. We ain't on that. We just here to have a good time," he told them.

"Nigga, I didn't ask you shit, and I know you ain't on shit!" Freebandz barked, while staring down Asad like he was a punk.

"What the fuck! Nigga, you don't want it with me!" Asad replied and then took a step closer. "This ain't that! If this bitch with you, then take her dumb ass on!" he told him, pointing at Summer and now knowing that it was not a game.

Boony instantly exploded out of the crowd and charged at Asad with his head down like a bull. Asad pushed China out of the way as he quickly side-stepped him. He then hit Boony in the face with a hard knee that sent him crashing to the floor dazed and bloody. Seeing him go down made the other three goons rush in. China grabbed the Grey Goose bottle from the bar and hit the closest one with it and dropped him as well. Then she went after Summer, who had tried to get out of the way of all the drama that she had caused.

Freebandz snaked Asad from behind with a hard-right cross that almost knocked him off his feet. As soon as Eshy saw him stagger, he kicked Asad's legs out from under him. When Asad hit the floor, he was kicked in the face and then stomped by the others

17

until the club's bouncers and the police joined in to break up the beating. China had to be pulled off of Summer and held back from trying to help Asad. Once the police had the club cleared and a man in handcuffs—who had nothing to do with the fight—Asad was rushed by ambulance to the hospital.

~ ~ ~

It was another busy night in the emergency room at St. Joe's as the paramedics rushed Asad in on a gurney. They explained what was going on with him as they were escorted to a hospital room.

"He has swelling in his head. I believe it might be bleeding of his brain. We have to relieve the pressure if we're going to save this man's life," a nurse explained to a doctor as they both disappeared behind a closed door.

Chapter 3

Jasso paid the cabdriver once he made it to his destination. He then grabbed the bags and followed his wife into the busy airport ticket counter.

"Welcome to Mitchell Field. How may I help you?" the black male clerk asked the couple in Spanish.

"Hi! You should have two first-class tickets on hold for Mr. and Mrs. Rivera," Amanda replied in English with a smile, letting the young man know she approved of his Spanish.

"Alright! Let's see here." He tapped a few buttons on his keyboard. "Yes! Here it is. Let me just print it out for you."

He handed her the tickets and bid them a safe trip.

Jasso looked at the time and noticed that they only had a few minutes to burn before they had to be on the plane.

"I need to find a quick drink!"

"No, baby. Look! The plane is boarding now," Amanda informed him, looking at the departure board. "We can get something to eat and drink on the plane. I don't wanna lose our seats," his wife continued, pulling him by the hand toward the gate.

"Mandy, we can't lose our seats. It's an airplane, not a Greyhound bus."

Jasso didn't like flying and needed a drink to help relax him.

"Whatever! I know what it is!" she playfully hit him.

He knew it would be better for him if he just gave her what she wanted and got drunk on the flight. They found their seats on the port side of the plane. First class was much roomier than coach, which made it a little better on his nerves; and just as his wife had promised, drinks were served. When the flight attendant came by, they ordered drinks, sandwiches, and apple pie for dessert. The lovebirds finished their meal and held hands as they laughed at a movie with the Rock playing an oversized tooth fairy.

Although Jasso smiled and relaxed, the alcoholic beverages did nothing to take his mind off the car that chased him the other day. When the movie ended, he put his head back and went to sleep. It didn't seem like he was out long before Amanda woke him up in the bright sunny state of California.

When they picked up their luggage, Amanda's dad was there to pick them up.

"Hey, Papa!" she yelled, giving the old man a big hug.

"How was the flight? Was first class all I said it would be?"

"Yeah, it was nice. But I still don't like being up there," Jasso answered while shaking his father-in-law's hand and then allowing him to help put the bags in the trunk of the gold Lincoln Town Car.

Jasso sat in the back of the car, so Amanda could talk with her dad in front as he drove them home.

~ ~ ~

As soon as Ms. King read the text China had sent her about her son, she dressed and rushed to be at his side. When she made it to the busy hospital, she found the first nurse who could give her Asad's room number. As she walked down the hall, Ms. King heard China calling her name.

"Hey! How is he?" she asked, giving the distressed young woman a much-needed hug.

"I don't know nothing yet. They're still in there working on him. I tried to get in there, but they wouldn't let me."

"Where is he?" Ms. King asked, taking hold of China's shaking hands.

"Down here!"

China then led the way to the room and looked through the window at the medical personnel working hard to save Asad's life.

"Excuse me, but you can't be here. You've got to wait in the family waiting area until someone comes for you," a nurse walked up and informed them, before she went inside and closed the curtains.

They spent the next half hour in the waiting room hoping a doctor would come tell them what was going on. Ms. King closed her eyes and said a quick prayer for her only living child.

Her first born was killed at the age of thirteen by a drunk driver. The man fell asleep behind the wheel of his 1979 Ford pickup that jumped the curb too fast for her son to get out of the way. He was smashed against the wall of the corner store on 16th and Locus Street and died instantly. Linda King gave birth to Asad two years later.

Because of the almighty social media networks, the news of what happened at the club spread through the city like a wildfire. Some posts said that Asad had gotten stabbed and died on his way to the hospital. Others said he was in the hospital on life support. All these posts flooded China's cell phone, which were soon followed by so many concerned calls and texts that she had to power off her phone to get a break.

Before this day, China had never attended church with Ms. King. But with true faith, she got down with her and prayed alongside her as Asad's mother offered her life to save her son.

A doctor soon emerged from the room and

22

walked over to the nurses' station.

"I think the doctor just came out of Asad's room, ma," China said to Ms. King, who jumped from her seat and joined China, who was standing at the door of the waiting room.

When the mother saw the doctor start walking their way, with a nurse following close behind him, she feared the worst. "How is he?" she demanded with a shaky voice filled with fear.

"We were able to stop the bleeding successfully, but he is still non-responsive," the doctor said. He looked from one face to the other. "I've done all I can do for him at this time."

"What the fuck do that mean?" China asked, feeling as if the doctor was giving up on Asad.

"Well, ma'am. First, calm down! All I'm saying is that I can't do more until he wakes up," the tired-looking doctor explained.

"Can we see him now?" Ms. King asked.

"Right now, he's in the recovery room, but as soon as he's moved to the coma ward, you can see him."

"Coma?" was all China got out before she took a step and passed out.

The nurse and Ms. King tried to catch her, but all they were able to do was fall with her to the floor.

Chapter 4

Still agitated over Jasso getting away from them the other day—and amped up on pills, weed, and alcohol—the hot-headed heathens went on a robbing spree across the city. It was open season on everything and almost everyone. They hit cabdrivers and corner hustlers standing out on blocks. They went after pretty much anyone who could add to their hollow pockets.

These small licks weren't enough for Eshy, however; he needed much more. He had a wifey and a new set of twin boys at home to feed, and they were behind on everything right now. Just that day his girl received a thirty-day notice for them to pay the past due rent they owed or move out of their apartment.

"Eshy, they said it's a big gamble that's supposed to be going down on the east side," Boony said while driving up north in search of a good lick.

"When is this?" asked Freebandz as he loaded a blunt with some kush they got off one of the dope boys they had robbed.

"Tonight! I think it's over by Palmar and Wright. I'm not sure, but it shouldn't be hard to find. All we gotta do is look for all the whips and whatever spot has a lot of in-and-out traffic."

"Stop talking about it, fam, and let's get it. If it ain't going down, there's always something sweet we can hit on the east side," Eshy said as the Impala changed directions and now headed down North Avenue toward the east side of the city.

~ ~ ~

The doorbell rang and was opened by three treacherous men. Boony grabbed the guy who opened the door by the face, and slammed him into the door as it closed. But it was the boom of Freebandz's gun that made the whole house stop and pay attention.

"All you muthafuckas, get the fuck down!" Eshy commanded waving his gun. "Throw down your phones, bling, everything. Empty your fucking pockets! I want it all! And look at the floor, or all you bitches are going to end up like your guy!" he ordered as he pointed at the dead doorman.

Boony made sure to take the dead man's gun just in case somebody wanted to play hero. Then he helped Freebandz search the house for valuables and to make sure no one was hiding. Boony took a pillowcase from one of the beds before rejoining the team.

"Put everything in the bag now, bitch!" Eshy ordered a female, who looked way too young to be in the house with everyone.

When she was done, he told her to lie down on the floor where she stood. The three of them then made their way back out the same way they had entered. Freebandz shot the already dead man again on the way out just to remind everyone to stay where they were until they were gone. Eshy drove as the others rummaged through the pillowcase and extracted all the cash, drugs, and jewelry.

"How much cash is it?" Eshy asked after they were safely out of the area.

"It looks like about fifty or sixty Gs, give or take!" Boony estimated while trying on a gold Cartier watch from the bag.

Eshy did a quick calculation in his head. He felt he knew his men better than they knew themselves.

"Hey, y'all. Take a ten apiece, and then divide the jewelry, all except that one bracelet—the rainbow-colored joint. I need that. My bitch's birthday's coming up!"

"That's cool!" Boony agreed, looking for the bracelet that Eshy was talking about and handing it to him.

"E! What we gonna do about the work?" Freebandz asked, already making plans for many of the drugs he held in his hands.

"What you mean, fam? We're going to party with that shit," Eshy answered, pulling over in the middle of a bridge on 39th and Cherry.

"Hand me all them phones. We don't need that bullshit with us, because they can track some of them joints."

"Fo' sho'! But we can't party with all this here. Let me flip some of this shit, E," Freebandz said while bumping out everything from the pillowcase and putting the cell phones back in it before he handed it to Eshy.

"Good thinking, my nig! Do what you do!" Eshy told him as he got out of the car and bumped the pillowcase over the side of the bridge.

Chapter 5

On the third day at the hospital, Ms. King made China go home to get herself together. "You should go home and get you some rest, China. You look a mess! You know Asad wouldn't want you looking like this."

"Ma, I want to be here when he wakes up. He needs to know I'm here with him no matter what," she pleaded.

"Girl, he knows that already. You're the only one I've ever known to do so much for him and trust him enough to consider moving in with him."

"He told you he wants to move in with me?" China smiled for the first time since they got to the hospital.

"Yeah, he did, but don't tell him I told you that. Now go home! I promise to call you if anything happens while you're gone. And, China, have you called your job? You need to let them know what's going on. You don't need to get fired."

"I'm going to call them as soon as I get home. I'm taking his clothes and stuff home. I'll bring him something else to wear."

The two hugged, and China kissed Asad's dry lips before she left the hospital.

~ ~ ~

On the way home, she turned on both of his cell phones, and within seconds, the phones were flooded with text alerts. China read the last one that came in because it was from Sky. China had always been curious about the relationship between Sky and her man.

She saw that it was Sky begging for him or China to get in touch with her to let her know what was going on with him. China knew Sky must have read some of the speculations people were posting about the fight at the club and Asad's condition afterward, so she called Sky back from Asad's phone.

"Hello? Asad? Who is this?" Sky answered right away.

China could hear the worry in her voice.

"This is Asad's wife. Is this Sky?"

"Yes. Hey, is he alright? Because Facebook be full of shit. I don't wanna believe nothing on it."

"I don't know what all you heard, but he's not dead. He's in the hospital still."

China went on and told Sky about his condition and what really went down the night at the club.

"All I know is when I walked out of the bathroom, this high-yellow bitch was all in Asad's face. So I asked him who she was, and the nappy-headed bitch tried to pop slick with me getting all loud and shit. That's when some niggas that must've been with her came talking shit. Then, for no reason, one of them rushed Asad and got dropped. That's when the rest of them jumped him. I hit one of them in the head with a bottle before I went after that bitch. The next thing I knew, the bouncer had me in a bear hug and let that hoe get away. When I made the punk put me down, I saw Asad lying on the floor covered in blood," she explained, getting mad at herself all over again for asking to go to that club.

"Hey, China, I know the timing is fucked up right now, but I need to talk to you in person about my thing with Asad. Feel me?"

China knew what she was talking about, so she told her to meet her in the upper-level cafeteria of the mall when she got home. China knew Asad often met people like this, so she felt it was okay to do. She knew better than to bring one of his friends or the street life into their home.

~ ~ ~

Once she got home, she showered and dressed in a Juicy Couture warm-up suit and matching Air Max running shoes. China didn't feel like doing anything but being at the hospital with her man. Just like she promised, Ms. King texted her and let her know that nothing had changed. Ms. King also told her to try not to worry because they had to be strong for him. The text ended with her telling China to say a prayer for him and to get some rest before she came back. China texted back and told her to tell Asad that she loved him, and she reminded Ms. King to contact her if anything new happened with him.

After making calls to her job and returning calls from friends and family, it was time for her to meet up with Sky. China said a quick prayer for Asad before she walked out the door of her apartment to meet Sky. China found her standing in front of the Subway, where they both ordered food and sat down to eat and talk, away from the crowded tables in the food court.

"Have you heard anything new about Asad?" Sky asked, before taking a bite of her sub.

"Mama texted me not long ago and said he was the same."

To China's surprise, tears started to burn her eyes as she thought of Asad lying helpless in the hospital bed. She quickly got it together in front of Sky, since she didn't want to seem weak to her.

"Boo, it'll be okay. I know he's a fighter, so he's going to come out of this shit soon. You don't gotta be ashamed to show your love for your man. Hell! To tell you the truth, a bitch been crying and worried sick ever since I heard about this shit with him!"

"I'm okay now," China said while blotting her eyes with a napkin.

Sky explained to her how she did things with Asad. A lot of it was what Asad had told China already, which made China feel bad about doubting him when he told her he was working. Sky was attractive with her tomboyish style. Her hair was in long dreads that she wore pinned up on top of her head, letting the rainbow-colored tips fall across her shoulders. This complimented her sexy dark skin and golden-brown eyes. She stood five foot nine and a half and weighed 150 pounds, but she was all legs and butt. Sky was bisexual, but at the time, she was sharing a small house with a sexy white girl named Penny from Madison, Wisconsin, who she was dating. Neither of them had children.

"I'm just about finished with the few pounds he gave me." Sky then handed China an envelope of cash. "There's six Gs in there. I'll bring you the rest when I'm done," Sky began before she paused for a moment.

"China, are you going to be around? I mean, are you going to be handling things until he gets out of the hospital? This shit's moving fast, and the last time I talked to him, he told me what he was trying to do. I promised to help, and I don't want to slow shit down."

"I know, Sky. But I have to be at the hospital with my bae, and I don't really know what to do."

"Why don't you just have everyone on his line call me and give me like ten at a time or even five. This way I can make sure things are right for the main man, and all you got to do is make sure the cash is right."

China thought on it for a quick minute. She knew what Sky was asking and that Asad trusted her. So she agreed and forwarded all Asad's calls to Sky's phone. China decided to only give her five pounds at a time, so she wouldn't lose count of how many pounds were out. The two ironed out a few more details while finishing their food, before they parted ways.

Once she arrived back in her apartment, China climbed into bed but couldn't get relaxed. She was just lying in the dark staring at the ceiling and hugging Asad's pillow. But soon the scent of her man, combined with her tired body, soothed her enough to allow sleep to take her.

In the morning, she awoke refreshed and then rushed back to the hospital so Ms. King could go home and get herself some rest as well. China took an overnight bag because she planned to go to work from the hospital the next day.

Chapter 6

A week after attending his sister-in-law's wedding, Jasso made it home only to find himself right back on the road to take care of his business with his connect. He took one of his young hot-headed Latin King brothers with him, named Zay. Jasso let him do most of the driving since Zay had so much energy. They made the trip by crossing the border into San Luis where the overworked and underpaid border patrol officers didn't mind turning a blind eye for the right price.

If it were anyone else crossing into Mexico, they would have had to show a visitor's pass. But Jasso was a guest of some very important people, and the place where he was going was outside of the central area, so cash was all the paperwork he needed.

The city was simple and small, as were many of the farms they passed. Jasso had already informed Zay that the city was not where they were going. This was Zay's first time in Mexico, so he took in everything and stored as much of it in his memory as he could.

"Bro, what the fuck is that shit up there?" Zay

asked as they came up to what looked to him to be a military roadblock.

"Nothing! Just relax, bro. They don't give a fuck about us or what we bringing in. They know it's money for one of the bosses, so they won't fuck with us. But every now and then, they get on some bullshit with what's being smuggled out. They'll take it and resell it to another muthafucka or extort you for more cash, knowing you don't wanna spend no time in their jails down here."

Jasso saw the concern on Zay's face.

"Don't trip! We good. We got a pass, so they can't fuck with us without suffering the consequences behind it," he tried to assure him.

"If you good, I'm good!" Zay told Jasso, trying his best not to make eye contact with any of the officers as he drove through.

They passed a big rig being searched by another set of patrol officers on the opposite side of the road.

"That's what happens when you don't got a pass!" Jasso explained, answering Zay's unasked question.

After driving a few more miles, they again started seeing more farms and buildings. Jasso informed him that they had made it to the place where they were supposed to go. He had Zay pull over next to the town's only convenience store in sight. This is where the meeting was set up to be held.

A broad-shouldered Mexican man looked up at them from his nap and waved them in toward him when they got out of the white Ford Expedition in which they were told to arrive. The man met them halfway from the truck to give them a quick pat down.

Another man who Jasso knew only as Luis appeared in the doorway. Luis's face was so sun-kissed that it made it hard to guess how old he was. He reminded Zay of the actor Danny Trejo. Luis welcomed them with a deep Spanish accent, but only offered Jasso his hand to shake.

"Who's your young friend?" he asked while looking suspiciously at Zay.

"He's cool. He's my driver."

But to show Luis that Zay was a team player, Jasso told him to hand Luis the money he had brought for them.

Luis smiled and accepted the duffle bag. He then looked inside before passing it to another one of his men, who walked up next to him.

"I'm sorry, my friend, but that's not good enough for me. I know you, but he could be anybody."

With that said, the man then patted them down and pressed a gun into Zay's ribs.

"How about you show me you can be trusted."

"Don't trip, bro! Remember, I told you this might happen."

Zay nodded and allowed the man to lead him into a garage next to the store. There was a bound and badly beaten man inside. Luis then pulled his gun from his waist and passed it over to Jasso. When Zay saw that, he smiled to himself since he knew what they wanted him to do.

"Have him kill him or lose both your lives," Luis ordered Jasso in Spanish.

"Here, homie. Do what you do best," Jasso ordered Zay.

This was also Jasso's way of seeing how the youngster held up under pressure. Jasso wasn't surprised when Zay took the gun and shot the man twice in the chest, before handing the gun back to Jasso. Jasso was proud he did it without question.

"Is that good?"

"Yes! Yes! Let's go inside so we can get you on your way," Luis answered, before turning and leading the way back to the store.

Once they stepped into the store, they saw the bag sitting on a scale just to the right of the entrance. They weighed money instead of counting it, because it saved time. The scale read 103.5 pounds. It wasn't until then that the conversation switched to English.

"Jasso, my friend, what you came all this way for is waiting for you neatly packed in the walls of the RV that you parked next to," Luis explained to them while pointing out the store's front window.

"Miguel here will make sure you and our new friend make it safely across the border, but that's as far as he goes. Boss's orders."

Luis pointed to a big, heavy-set man standing by the corner of the counter.

"Now we can work something out a little better for a nice price?"

"How much is that price?"

"Let's say another two Gs to make him happy to cross the state lines," Luis offered with a smile. "That will be better for you."

"Okay, I'll pay that!" Zay spoke up.

"Okay, it's a deal!" Jasso seconded his man's decision. "But, Luis, the next time you need someone to do your dirty work, it's going to cost you."

Zay was glad that Jasso didn't say no to it, because after he saw the way the police did things on the way in, he really did not want to be bothered with them. Also, with Miguel driving the RV, he could get some rest before he had to take the wheel.

Zay told Jasso that he could pay Miguel out of the money he was getting for making the trip with him. Zay knew if all went well, he would be Jasso's new right-hand man, and money would not be an issue.

Little did the youngster know that he had already gotten the position. He had been chosen as soon as he pulled the trigger earlier in the day. Jasso vowed the day that he was followed by the Impala not to move around alone until he found out who tried to follow him. And he wanted to know if they had anything to do with what had happened to Asad.

Chapter 7

Many relate smells of chlorine and other disinfectants in a hospital with death. So Ms. King, other loving family members, and friends had filled Asad's room with the sweet scent of flowers. His room was always cool and quiet, except for the electronic beeping sound from the machines to which Asad was hooked up.

It had now been just under three weeks since that tragic night that put Asad in his long restful state. Sky had started taking turns sitting with him since China and his mom both had jobs. She had just made it there when she saw his hand move.

"Ma, he just moved his hand! He just moved it for real!" she said, stopping Ms. King from walking out of the door.

She rushed over to her son's side just in time to hear him try to speak.

"Wake up, Asad! Mama's here, baby! Wake up! It's okay. Just open your eyes," she encouraged him with tears running down her face while she held his hand tightly.

Sky shed tears of joy herself as she quickly

pressed the nurse's call button with one hand and texted China with the other. When she didn't get a response from China right away, she called her phone, which sent her straight to voicemail.

Immediately, a doctor and two nurses ran in and had the two women leave the room after they explained that Asad had moved his hand and whispered something they could not make out. But Ms. King saw Asad open his eyes just as the door was closed in her face.

"I can't get China on the phone. I texted and called her, but I was sent to voicemail."

"Okay, let me call her job. She might be away from her cell phone."

When Ms. King called her job, they told her China had just gone home for a family emergency.

"Sky, I think she's on her way. Her job just said she left for a family issue. I hope this is the reason China took off from work, because that girl don't need no more on her plate."

~ ~ ~

Just as they had hoped, China was on her way to the hospital. She was about to take a break at work when she read Sky's texts, so she hurried and clocked out. Everyone at her job was aware of Asad's condition and was praying for him to get better, so no one questioned her when she had to leave.

China found everyone in the waiting room. The doctor had just walked up looking for them, to explain what was going on with Asad.

"Hi, I'm Dr. Jamison. You're the mom, right?" he asked Ms. King.

From the smile on his face, Ms. King knew it was good news.

"Yes! Is he alright?"

"Well, he's awake and reasonably sound. I'm listing him in stable condition, but that doesn't mean he's out of the woods, because eighteen days is a pretty long time to be out. I'm going to be doing some more tests, and I want to keep a close eye on him for the next few days. I know all of you want him to get well soon." The doctor paused a moment. "I don't want to stress him, so I'm only allowing him two visitors max at any time."

The doctor was paged to the nurse's station, so once the family members agreed, Dr. Jamison rushed off.

"Let me go in alone with my baby first. I have to go home and get some rest before work," Ms. King said as she turned to China. "Missy, you make sure I'm the first to know if anything happens to him while I'm gone."

"Yes ma'am. You know I will," China promised, wishing she could go in with her to see Asad as well.

42

But she knew how scary this had been for them all, and she knew whatever Ms. King had to say was for her son's ears only.

"Mama?" Asad said weakly when he saw her walk through the door and close it behind her.

"Yeah, baby? I'm here."

She walked over and sat down next to his bed.

"Why am I here? The doctor wouldn't tell me. What's going on?"

"Asad, let's not think about that right now. He didn't tell you because he don't want you to stress yourself, and he just told us out there not to do the same. You just try to rest so you can get out of here."

She took his hand right away, noticing it was much warmer than it had been.

"Do you need anything to drink or some of these ice chips, because I don't think you can have water just yet."

"Yeah, some ice chips. Everything is dry and sore," he told her before he coughed weakly.

Ms. King lovingly hand-fed her son the ice chips and openly thanked God for giving him back to her. About ten minutes later, she returned to the waiting room to find Penny had now joined China and Sky.

"Hey y'all! He's all yours now!" she greeted them as they all got up from their seats and met her at the entrance.

"How's he doing?" China and Sky asked almost

at once.

"Did he ask about me?" China nervously asked.

Ms. King let out a little chuckle at the way they were acting.

"He doing good. Still a little tired, but he's up and talking. When you go in there, make sure he eats some more of that ice, because his throat's still sore from the tubes and not using his voice for so long."

"I'll make sure he does that, mama," China assured Ms. King.

"Did he say anything about what happened to him that night?" Sky questioned.

"No, and I didn't ask. He don't know how he got to the hospital, and I don't want none of you telling him about it either. I talked to Dr. Jamison again, and he said Asad may have some memory loss, and only time will tell how much and how long it will last. We all got to keep praying for him." She pulled on her jacket and took out her car keys. "When you go in there, don't push him too hard," she warned.

"I'll walk you out to your car since only two of us can go in to see him," Penny told Ms. King, who then put on her things and walked her out of the waiting area toward the parking garage.

China hesitated a moment when they reached Asad's room door. She and Sky both took a few breaths to try to shake their nerves before entering the room. Sky knocked lightly, and then they went

44

in. The first thing she noticed was that he was no longer hooked up to the respirator, but he was still hooked up to the IV and heart monitor.

"Hey, y'all!" he greeted with a big smile. The two love-struck women returned the smile as they walked over and took up places on opposite sides of the bed. Asad was sitting up in the bed with two flat pillows behind him. They knew his mom had done her best to make him comfortable before she went home. His head was poorly shaven and wrapped in bandages, and so was his chest. Sky wanted badly to throw her arms around him and cover his face with kisses, but she knew it was not the right time to express just how she felt. She did not want to disrespect China in any way or let her know that she was in love with Asad.

China kissed him and told him that he had to eat some ice chips before they got to talking too much. Then she went against Ms. King and the doctor's orders and asked him a bunch of little questions just to see how bad his memory loss might be. It was a trick she picked up during her time working with the elderly.

"I guess my mother told y'all not to tell me how I got here with my head and shit all wrapped the fuck up, right?"

"You got it, buddy. So, don't ask! Just try to give these doctors what they need so they can let you go home, where China can take care of you the right way."

"Yeah, and home will be my place! So, tell me what you need, and I'll have it there for you. This is not up for debate, Asad!" China told him, taking advantage of what she wanted.

He agreed without a fight, but they could tell he was trying hard to remember something.

China guessed it was where he lived in the first place. Sky thought he was trying to figure out what their relationship was to him.

After a few more minutes, the nurse came in and told them that visiting hours were over. But by then Asad had fallen asleep, and they were just watching over him like two mothers in a nursery watching over a newborn child.

Chapter 8

Jasso sweet-talked his way past the intake desk. He had the freckle-faced, full-figured redhead smiling as he promised to hook up with her on her day off, in return for her giving him the afterhours pass to visit his brother. Asad was asleep when he got to the room. Not wanting to have come all this way for nothing, Jasso woke him up.

"Hey, wake your punk ass up, bro! Ain't shit wrong with you no more!" he joked, slapping the side of the bed.

Asad was startled awake. The television was the only light in the room, but he recognized his friend right away.

"Man, fuck you and your wake-up call! Go away! You just fucked up a good-ass dream!" he told him as he raised the bed and turned the light on in the room.

Jasso laughed as he leaned over the bed.

"You look like shit, bro! I'm going to have to buy you a wig before I take you anywhere with me."

"Fuck you, funny man! How long you been here?" Asad looked at the clock on the wall next to the door. It read 12:37 a.m. "And how did you get in here? I thought visiting hours was over?"

"Let me guess. You don't wanna see me?"

They laughed.

"Bro, I told the big bitch at the desk I'll let her suck me off for free if she lets me see my long-lost brother from another muthafucka."

The two laughed some more.

"But on the real, bro-bro, how you doing?"

"I'm good, I guess. Things are a little foggy, but I'm good."

They shook hands.

"I don't know why I'm here, and can't believe that I've been here almost a month."

Asad shook his head at the thought.

"They said I'll be good to get out of here in a few days if I can keep my food down and shit. Then I'll see what's really good because won't nobody tell me shit."

"Well, bro! You won't get anything out of me. I don't know much anyway. But I do know that your moms don't want us talking to you about nothing. I got that warning from your wifey."

"Wifey? Oh, you talking about China, right?"

"Yeah, fool! Do you got one I don't know about?" Jasso joked, not knowing that Asad really didn't know who he was referring to. "You got a good one there, bro. She's been holding shit down and doing her thang for you. Hell, I think China's moving them so good, I don't need you no more," he joked.

"I didn't know she was fucking with you like that. Her and Sky told me they was taking care of my bill, that's all. I didn't know what the hell they were talking about."

"On some real shit, bro. We gotta holla about some shit later. Right now, you just get better quick because we got work to do, and I want them niggas that put you in here." Jasso knew he had said too much as soon as it came out of his mouth.

"Man, I don't even know what you're talking about. I can't remember shit really. I remember sitting in a car with you, and pretty much everything else after that is a blank."

"I guess that's to be expected since you was in a coma. Bro, it is natural for you to be out of it for a minute. What was it like?"

"I don't know! I guess it was like being in a long-ass dream but realer. I saw my big brother. We were sitting in a park talking about everything."

"I didn't know you had a brother."

"Yeah, I did, but he died before I was born. I only saw him on photos that moms got around the house. She told me about him, but I don't remember her telling me shit about a park. My brother looked just like my pops and shit. The only thing I remember him telling me was to wake up, and I did."

"That's some real shit, bro-bro." Jasso looked at his watch. "Don't worry, my nig! You going to get it all back," he tried to assure Asad. "But I better get my pretty Mexican ass up out of this bitch before Amanda gets on one with me."

"Or ol' girl at the desk gets off work and makes you pay up," Asad teased.

"Love, bro!"

"Almighty!" Asad responded as they shook hands.

Jasso slipped back out the way he came in, rushing to get home before he got put in the dog house or his wife put him in a bed next to Asad.

Chapter 9

Penny carefully navigated her yellow Ford Escape home after she and Sky finished knocking off their to-do list. They were coming from Sam's Club when she noticed how quiet Sky was. She hadn't said much since they made it home last night after Asad awoke from his coma. Penny knew something was wrong with Sky because she was not smoking, and Sky usually had a blunt lit up from sunup to sundown every day.

"What do you got a taste for tonight?"

"I'm not really all that hungry, and I don't feel like going out. So, babe, let's just chill at home," Sky suggested.

"Okay, bae. Hey, light that half a blunt up for me?" Penny asked, pointing to the ashtray as she drove.

She hoped the smell of it would pull Sky out of her dull mood. But it didn't work, so she had to finish it by herself.

Once they got all the bags in the house, Penny took Sky by the hand and pulled her into their bedroom. The weed Penny smoked had her horny, and she did her best to let Sky know it.

Sky felt Penny's eyes caress her, and for the first time, she noticed Penny had on the perfume she gave her for her birthday. It always made Sky's blood rush. She slowly melted into her lover's arms as Penny pulled her in, before sucking on her lower lip and then kissing her.

"Baby, I know you're in a mood about your friend. No! I really know how you feel about him, and I'm cool with it. Asad was a part of you way before I came along. But, Sky, since he's been in the hospital, you haven't been the same. I miss you!"

It had been weeks since they touched each other, and Penny wasn't taking no for an answer tonight.

"Pen, I just!"

"No, Sky. Please don't push me away tonight," she begged, before she kissed her cheek, tasting the salt from Sky's earlier tears.

"I'm sorry, baby. This has just been hell on me," she murmured into Penny's neck as she began to nibble on her soft strawberry skin.

They shed their clothes in an awkward lustful tangle, helping one another along the way. Penny's pale skin flushed with anticipation that was quickly building inside her. When Sky was naked, she pushed her down on the bed breaking their kiss. Then Penny ran her hands teasingly up Sky's dark thighs, dropping to her knees at the same time. She first stroked Sky's silky folds with her long fingers and then followed them with her mouth.

Sky let her suck and lick on her until she felt her first wave building. But before she released, Sky pulled Penny away up over her so she could suck on a mouthful of her breast, just the way she knew Penny liked her to do. But Penny wasn't having it. She worked her way back down, kissing her lips, neck, breasts, and belly until she was back where she started.

"Cum for me, baby! Let mama have it!"

Sky loved the feeling of Penny's wetness as she humped and grinded against her leg. But soon her thoughts turned to Asad, and she flipped Penny over to switch places with her. Sky tongue-kissed Penny's dripping warmth while she pulled her big black dildo out from the nightstand.

They made love together on and off well into the night, with both of them getting lost in their passion.

~ ~ ~

Penny woke up to an empty house and a nice wad of cash on the nightstand beside her. She picked up her cell and saw that Sky had texted her:

"Good morning, sleepy head. I had to run to get this money and didn't want to wake you. It's the weekend, so you know how it can get for me. I don't want you to be sitting in the house, so I left you some cash to go out and have some fun."

This was right up her alley. Spending money was what she did best.

~ ~ ~

Penny wandered around Bay Shore Mall after getting her hair and nails done, before she decided to take the expressway and head to the casino to try her luck at the slots. Since it was still pretty early, she did not have to look hard for a good parking place. As soon as Penny walked through the door, she could feel the luck and anticipation thick in the air. She walked up to an empty blackjack table where the dealer was flipping himself cards as he waited for the rush that was sure to soon come.

Penny placed her money on the table.

"Do you need change, ma'am?" the dealer asked while fishing out a new deck of cards.

"No, play it all!"

"Okay, playing $100!" he called out, holding the bill to the light and then running a marker across it before putting it into play.

The dealer then shuffled the deck before he dealt Penny a queen of clubs and a ten of hearts. The dealer got a bust with an eight of hearts, a seven of spades, and a king of clubs, which quickly added to Penny's have-fun cash.

"Play it all! I came to have fun, win or lose! But mama's feeling lucky!" she said excitedly, jumping up and down like a kid.

Once again she hit.

"Winner!" the dealer called out as he passed her a bunch of blue chips.

Her luck soon brought over a small crowd to the table to watch the action and try to get in on her luck. Many of the gamblers were trying to pick up on Penny's winning secret. The pit boss sent her over free drinks and was also watching her play. Unbeknownst to her, she was also being watched by two notorious stickup kids who weren't doing well at the craps table. But seeing her winning the way she was, the two knew their luck had just changed.

"Fam, I'm about to go over to the slots so I can keep an eye on that bitch."

"Alright, my nig! Which ones, so I'll know where to find you when it's time to move."

"Them nickel joints over there," Eshy answered, pointing toward a bank of machines. "I'll text you if I move around from there. But you can believe I got my good eye on that snow bunny."

"For sure, family, I'ma try to get some of my loot back right here," Freebandz replied before he then rolled the dice that he was holding.

"Winner!" Eshy heard the dealer call out to him.

He knew his luck was now looking better and better. He smiled at his partner as he made his way to the slots.

~ ~ ~

Penny went home hours later feeling good with the $4,000 she had won at the casino. The only reason she left was because she wanted to share what she was feeling with Sky. For some reason, Penny thought of her mother's words when she first came out to her. Penny's mother had told her that a person knows that love is real when they want to spend every moment with that special someone and share both the good and bad with them.

As Penny walked from her car to the door of her home, she suddenly heard someone behind her.

"Who's that?" she questioned while looking back over her shoulder at the two men who seemed to appear from nowhere.

"Say, baby girl! I'm looking for 1841A. I'm late picking my son up from Ms. Pat. Do you know her?" Eshy asked.

He then quickened his step to catch up to her as he pretended to read the address from a piece of paper that he had ripped from a brown bag he found outside his car.

Penny tightened her hand on her keys and flipped

off the cap of pepper spray she kept on the key ring. Her mother had given her two of them a few months ago because she didn't like the north side of the city. Her mother always worried about Penny because of all the bad things she had watched on the news. But her daughter was grown and in love, so no one could tell her anything.

"No, you got the wrong house!"

"Okay, sexy! What's your name, or is your man in the house?" he asked.

However, before she could answer, Freebandz rushed up the stairs toward her.

Penny didn't hesitate spraying him, but she gasped as Eshy ducked and slid to her right. He grabbed her small wrist and twisted it as he took the keys and spray away from her.

"Open the door!" he ordered as he tossed her keys to Freebandz.

Eshy slapped Penny in the mouth hard covering her cry for help. She struggled and fought him while kicking wildly and trying to free herself. Eshy grunted when Penny bit the inside of his hand.

"It's open! Get that bitch in here!" Freebandz announced while still trying to clear the cheap spray off his face.

With the door open, Eshy forced Penny into the house.

"Bitch!" Freebandz yelled out before he punched

her in the stomach and face.

She dropped to her knees in pain, bloody and gasping for air yet at the same time fighting not to give in to the darkness.

"Folks, I'm going to fuck this bitch nice and hard since she likes it rough."

He undid his belt.

"Let's get what we came for first, and then see what else we can find in this bitch's place before we party this hoe."

Since they had way too much to drink and too many drugs in their system, they took turns beating and violating Penny. But before they made their getaway, Freebandz took a pillow from the sofa and placed it over the unconscious woman's face. He then pulled out his gun and shot her twice. He didn't want to be known as a rapist if she could remember his face and tell the police.

Chapter 10

Old Mrs. Summerville lived across the street from Sky and Penny. She quickly dialed 911 when she saw two men running from the house where the two young women lived together. She knew Sky wasn't home, because Mrs. Summerville had bought some weed from her. Sky had told her that she was going to be home late, but she would get her enough to last until morning. The old lady thought she had witnessed a break-in, but certainly not a rape and murder.

~ ~ ~

As soon as Sky hit the block, she saw the red and blue flashing lights. Then she noticed the news vans and the ambulance parked next to three unmarked police cars right outside her house. Sky's adrenaline rush blew her high as she jumped out of her car and ran to her house.

Everyone was out on their porches and standing around as she passed.

"What happened?" she asked when an officer

stopped her at the yellow warning tape.

"You have to stay back, ma'am!"

"I live here! What's going on? Where's Penny?" she demanded, quickly pushing past the officer.

"Hold up, ma'am! Let me call someone for you," he said as another officer walked over to escort her inside.

Her once immaculate living room now had a big black body bag lying in the middle of the floor and a big ugly bloodstain in the cream carpet.

"Somebody tell me where Penny is!" she demanded.

"They're going to talk to you right now, ma'am. You can ask the detective in charge."

The officer led her into the kitchen, where she was introduced to the person in charge.

The stone-faced detective asked a few choice questions about Sky and her relationship with Penny, before he told her that he believed Penny was the murder victim.

Sky's legs weakened, and someone caught her by the arm and helped her into a chair.

"How? I—I just talked to her. She was just so excited about something, and she told me she would be home when I got here. Penny told me that she'd be here," Sky repeated mostly to herself.

Then she got up and rushed out of the house avoiding looking at the body bag on the floor and refusing to let them see her break down.

~ ~ ~

Sky wandered the streets, just driving until she found herself in front of China's apartment.

"Please be home!"

China was awakened by the doorbell. She looked at the time on her phone that was lying in bed next to her, in case someone called about Asad. It was after 1:00 in the morning, but she got out of bed and went to the intercom.

"Yeah, who is it?"

"China, it's me. Let me in, please?"

"Okay, Sky, what's wrong?" she asked while buzzing her in.

China put on one of Asad's T-shirts, because she was asleep and only wearing a bra and panties. She then went to meet Sky at the elevator.

When the doors opened, Sky just stood there in shock biting her bottom lip. China pulled her into the apartment, at which time Sky was no longer able to hold back the tears burning in her eyes.

"Oh God, Sky, why are you crying?" she asked as they sat down on her leather sectional sofa.

"Penny's gone! She's dead! Some son of a bitch took her from me!"

"Oh no! No! What happened to her? What

happened to Penny, Sky?" she demanded as she wrapped her arms around her and let her own tears fall.

Sky told her all she knew from beginning to end. China did her best to console her friend. The past few weeks that Asad had been in the hospital brought them closer.

"Sky, I know it's painful for you right now, but I need you to take these. They will help you relax a bit," she explained as she handed her three sleeping pills and a glass of water.

Chapter 11

After being informed of the death of a close friend, the doctor agreed to let Asad go home. However, he made him promise to follow strict orders of bed rest for at least two more weeks and then return for a checkup.

Knowing Sky was crushed inside Asad felt it was best to give her time to herself before he went to see her. China stopped at her house to check on her on her way to work or home. Asad knew this, so he felt calling her here and there was good enough for the time being. He wanted to give her something the police had been unable to. He vowed to handle the individuals responsible for taking Penny's life, so Asad and Jasso put up $10,000 a piece on the heads of those involved.

~ ~ ~

Asad was home a week, but he was growing tired of sitting around the apartment gaming with faceless friends online. He felt a little claustrophobic, and he wondered if this was something he had dealt with before everything happened to him. He was a street boss and could no longer take sitting around waiting for his girl to get home from work. So Asad dressed in a dark gray and maroon Akoo outfit with matching Air Max 90s. After looking in the mirror, he decided he would go get a haircut in the mall. While in the barber chair, he felt the need to go to the storage building about which his mother had texted him.

Back in the apartment he grabbed a box of things that he did not need at the time. But doing this felt familiar to him as did the urge to have his own money. He took some cash from the apartment, that China had left for him to order delivery if he wanted something different to eat than what was in the refrigerator.

~ ~ ~

Taking a cab ride reminded Asad of how he never traveled the same route to the self-storage unit or home. What he didn't remember was the three water- and tamper-proof lockboxes safely tucked away in there. He used to add to the boxes once a week, nothing less than $5,000. His mother was the only person he trusted with knowing that he kept his money there. But even she didn't know how much was there. Asad had saved over $300,000.

He now sat trying to remember what pulled him

to this place. He took out a folding chair and just stared at all the boxes, trying hard to remember what was so important in the unit. After almost an hour of rummaging through stuff with no luck in remembering what he needed, Asad locked up the unit and then pulled his car out from another one.

He felt good to be back behind the wheel of his 1972 Pontiac Grandville. It was painted candy walnut with a blood-red and gold interior, and sat on 26" rims. In fact, it was the only thing that China knew was in storage. He remembered having her drive him to pick it up or drop it off. But as soon as he saw the car, he knew it was his. However, he still couldn't shake the feeling that he was still missing something as he pulled off in traffic.

He remembered how he would just cruise the city as rapper Alley Boy's hit song "Alone" pounded out of the four 15" subwoofers and ten 5.5" Kicker components that he used to compliment the deep bass.

~ ~ ~

China was surprised to see the big Pontiac in the parking space.

"My baby's back!" she said excitedly to herself.

She wore a big smile as she walked into the elevator, and when she reached her floor, she found the door unlocked. Her smile widened when she walked inside to find that the apartment had been cleaned. She then noticed the soulful voice of Tyrese in the background and the spicy smell of dinner in the air.

"Hey, my beautiful! Why you looking like that?" he greeted her while taking the pepper steaks from the warm oven.

"Well, damn! If this is what I get to come home to, I should get called in to work more often."

"Whatever!"

He kissed her.

"Go get yourself together, girl. You smell like old people, and I'm already to eat," he told her, giving her butt a squeeze before he let her out of his arms.

"Not so fast, Mr.! Who cooked this?" she questioned, popping a small piece of meat in her mouth.

"I did!" he lied with a smile.

"What the fuck ever, Asad! Who you get to cook this for you, because your ass can't cook minute rice!"

She stood there with a scolding look on her face.

"Okay, bae, you got me! Don't make that face. I got it to go from downstairs," he admitted to her.

"From Applebee's?" she asked over her shoulder, on her way to the bedroom to get cleaned up and changed.

The fresh haircut didn't escape her either. China had missed him getting all fresh and clean for her.

~ ~ ~

Just like before the coma, the young lovers cruised the city after dinner. They shared a blunt of some of Jasso's finest kush while letting themselves get lost to the sounds of Drake.

"Have you talked to Sky?" China asked while muting the song.

"No, not today. I'm giving her time to herself. Sky will come around when she's good or call when she needs us. I did talk to her sister though."

"What she say?"

"Shit, Tonya was talking about having the carpet changed in the house."

"Why? They did a great job cleaning it."

"Maybe, but their family's real superstitious and shit. She said she had Penny's things shipped to her family."

"So Sky is staying in that house?" China asked in surprise.

"Yep! You know she owns the place and don't want anyone in it right now," he answered while taking a hit off the blunt.

"Wow! I wish she wouldn't stay there. I couldn't do it!" she admitted, taking the weed and then a deep pull herself. Smoking was something China rarely did working in the nursing field, but she needed to let her hair down just for today. "I think you should go over there, bae. It might make her feel better seeing you out of the house."

"Right now?"

"No, not right this minute. But you should go see her later, after you take me home. I got to work, and from the looks of your smile, you're enjoying being out. So go see her. She needs to talk."

Asad agreed and then unmuted the sounds as he mashed on the gas, which sent them floating through the east side. He turned on Keefe Avenue to swing by and see a few guys he knew on 12th Street. At the stoplight on 8th, his old friend, D. Byrd, pulled up on him in a white-on-white Range Rover.

"What it do, bro! It's good to see you. Muthafuckas made it sound like you was dead or shit!"

"Now you know the real don't die that easy, my nig!"

"Right, right! I ain't going to hold you and your lady up. How you doing, Ms. Lady?"

China waved.

"I'll hit you up later. Is your line still the same?" D. Byrd asked.

"Yeah it's still that 610 one for a second. Hit me up. I may have something good for you. You still fool with that white, right?"

"Oh, you know it. Just hit me!" D. Byrd said, before he pulled off fast and let his big rims float and his bass pound.

The hood was live as always, and everyone showed Asad love as he slid through. He zig-zagged his way up in the numbers. They passed D. Byrd again; only this time he had a train of custom cars and trucks behind him. All the hood-rich brothers were out showing off in the streets. Asad saw that they even had the big homie Assa out in his tapped-out red and orange Chevy Monte Carlo.

After making a circle back down to the lakefront Asad took his girl home so she could get in a nap before work.

"See you later. You better call me and let me know you're alright. And go see Sky," China reminded him, before she gave him a hug and kiss and stepped out of the car.

"Love you!" he called out behind her as she walked through the doors of the mall.

He pulled off, picked up his cell, and texted Sky: "What up, love? Where you at? I'm out and trying to swing down on you."

"At the crib. Come on through," came her reply.

"Do you need anything from the store. I gotta pick up some blunts and something to drink."

"Bro, you must've forgot that I keep blunts. Just

grab me any kind of juice."

"Okay see you in a few."

Their text stream then ended.

Chapter 12

Sky shook off her thoughts of her lost love as she stepped out of the hot shower. She promised herself she would not cry anymore when she thought of Penny, and that she would tell Asad how she felt about him when he got there, because time isn't promised to anyone.

Her thoughts were interrupted by the sound of her front door being opened and closed. Sky froze in her tracks, still dripping wet from the shower.

"Skylar, where you at?"

She relaxed when she heard Asad's voice.

"I'm just getting out of the shower. I'll be right out."

"Alright, but why you have this door unlocked?" he asked, taking a seat on her new sofa set.

"I knew you were on your way."

"But still! You keep this muthafucka locked!"

"Don't trip! I got my tramp in here with me. A bitch ain't going easy, know that!" She hurried and dried herself. "But I'm going to give you a key just in case, alright?"

"That's cool."

She walked naked into her bedroom over to her lingerie drawer. She dressed as quickly as she could, and then put her .357 Magnum in the drawer beside her bed, knowing she did not need it with Asad being there.

"Hey you!" she greeted when she found him in her living room breaking down blunts for them.

"Hey, sis, how you feeling?"

"I'm getting there. I see you looking good and feeling better since you've been all out in the streets and shit."

"Sky, you know this shit don't stop for us. I gotta get it when it's there to be got, feel me?"

Asad's new look was turning her on. Gone were his long braids. He now wore a low brush cut. You could barely see the scar in his head, which she noticed had healed nicely.

"Asad, I want to tell you something!" she blurted out.

"Okay, you know you can tell me whatever, sis."

He passed her a blunt to light up.

Sky lit it and took two good pulls.

"I love you!" she admitted.

"I love you too."

"No, Asad. Don't say shit. Just let me finish." She hit the weed again and then continued: "I've always had feelings for you. I know you're with China, and I'm not trying to come between that or nothing. I just wanted you to know how I feel about you before something else happens to us." Sky paused to look in his face. "You don't gotta say shit. I just had to tell you." Right then, she broke her promise and let tears race down her face. "After what happened to Penny, I just had to tell you."

Asad put his arms around her not really knowing what to say. During the years they had known one another, he thought of her a few times sexually, but he quickly pushed those thoughts to the back of his mind, not wanting to damage their friendship. His feelings were just as real for her as they were for China.

Sky held on to him tightly while crying into his chest and taking in his scent.

"It's okay, Sky. Let it all out."

His cell beeped, which broke up the moment that was building between them. Asad knew it was a text, so he looked and saw it was from China.

"Hey! Just checking in on you. I'm going to bed. So you know if I don't answer the phone, that's why. Love you!"

"I'm good. Here with Sky. Love you too," he texted back.

When he put his phone down, Sky looked into his eyes and kissed him on the lips. She hoped he wouldn't pull away from her, because this was what she felt she needed. Asad didn't stop her. He returned the kiss with just as much passion, and before long, their clothes were scattered across the floor.

"Touch me!" she whispered, placing his hand on her breast.

Sky ran her hand down his chest to the hard muscles in his stomach. She did all the things she had imagined the last time she was with Penny. Her body tingled with his every touch.

Asad then ran his strong hands across her big brown thighs and butt, and between her legs. Her breathing became shallow as he sucked on her erect nipples and their fingers played tag between her thighs.

Sky climbed on top of him and slid his hardness all the way in her.

"Oh God! Yes! Yes, baby! I need this! I love you!" she moaned as she rode him.

Asad lifted her up and flipped her on her back, taking over the way he always thought of doing to her. He pounded her harder and harder inside until they came together with him buried deep inside of her. That moment changed the whole nature of their relationship.

Sky then got up and went into the bathroom. When she returned, she brought him a warm soapy wash cloth.

"You better get up and get dressed, so you can get home," she said as she washed him up. "Don't worry! This never happened."

"What if I want it to happen?"

He pulled her toward him and kissed her deeply. He then pushed her back on the floor and buried his head between her legs. Asad licked and sucked on her until he tasted her cum again. As Sky came for the second time, he once again filled her with his thickness.

Asad awoke hours later in Sky's bed. He woke her up and told her that he had to go home. He then got out of bed to get dressed. He told her to make sure she got up and locked the door behind him. Sky stopped him and gave him her spare key and a kiss to go.

Asad then walked out thinking that he loved both China and Sky, but each of them for different reasons. But the love for them was all the same. He lit up a blunt once he was in his car and changed the CD to Alisha Keys, so she could help him find his way through the maze in his heart.

Chapter 13

Park Lawn is a low-income housing project made up of brownstones and townhouses that stretch along Sherman Boulevard, starting on 43rd up to 47th and between Hope and Congress Streets. Inside this small subdivision of the city's many ghettos, Eshy, Boony, and Cash sat in the cool air-conditioned home of Freebandz and Summer, the mother of his two children and many times partner in crime.

"Eshy, man. I quit!" Cash announced after trying for over an hour and a half to win the money back he lost to him in a game of Wii Bowling.

"Oh! You running, fam? Tell me, is you running?" Eshy teased his friend while drinking a beer.

"Yeah! I'm running like the feds are behind my black ass!" he joked as he pressed the remote start of his black Chevy Camaro sitting on 22" black and chrome rims.

Cash wasn't a part of the team of thugs. He was the type that hung around them when they had money. Cash didn't care how they got paid as long as they spent some of it with him.

"It's all good, fam! Just give me five of them blue joints and we even!"

"Say no mo'! Here you go, and here's one for the road."

It was nothing for Cash to give up the pills. But it was cash that was hard for him to part with.

"Folks, if you can help us get that fool Jasso, we'll be good!" Boony spoke up out of nowhere.

"Man! Don't no muthafucka know where he stay. All bitches can tell us is that he's holding!" Freebandz added, taking Cash's place on the game.

"All I can tell is if the dude likes pussy, just find his bitch and make her take you to him!" Cash answered while looking out the door at a group of sluttishly dressed females standing by his car. "He got a bitch or two somewhere. Just find her, and y'all got him."

"Yeah, you right, my nig! I knew you was good for something!" Eshy agreed, downing his beer. "I think I know just where to look for her too."

Unknown to the others, he had been on the south side a few times since that day they lost Jasso, trying to find out how he got away from them.

"Well good. But I ain't going to keep giving y'all this game for free," Cash joked. "I'm out! I'll catch up with you fools in a bit. Summer, quit playing and put me in with that thick bitch you be kicking it with."

"Who, Forever?"

"Yeah, if that's her name. All I know is that hoe got money, and I love her for it."

"I got you, Cash. Just be there tonight," Summer reminded him to meet her at her job.

With that, Cash got in his car and let the bass from the hit song "Bandz" rattle the project windows before he peeled off.

~ ~ ~

Eshy took his younger cousin, Manace, and Boony with him over to the south side. Manace was always causing trouble by trying to show Eshy he was just as much a goon as he was. So Eshy thought a simple snatch-and-grab would show just what his little cousin was made of.

The two thugs sat and watched Manace from their positions in the car as he followed a few steps behind the female who Eshy had noticed Jasso spending a lot of time talking to in the past. He stopped suddenly when a police wagon pulled over and stopped across the street from the restaurant into which she was going. Even though Manace badly wanted to prove himself, he knew he had to let her go for now.

"I almost had the bitch, but I couldn't grab her with them boys sitting over there," he explained once he was back in the car.

"Don't trip, cuz. You did right. They would've been on our asses fast as hell if somebody saw you and called for help. We know the bitch is at work now!" Eshy explained to Manace.

"So what, we just going to sit here and wait for her to get off work?" Boony asked, being a little annoyed with the thought.

"Fuck no! We going to come back later and catch her then!" Eshy answered him.

That's all Boony needed to hear for him to pull off.

"Let's go grab something to drink and put in the air."

"Cuz, my nigga got that bag. Some shit called cow's breath!" Manace interrupted while still trying to make the team.

"I ain't never heard of that shit. It better be right!" Boony warned him as he drove.

"It is, and I can get it for the low. Just take me to the hood, and I'll show you better than all the talking shit."

~ ~ ~

When they returned later as they had planned, they were all intoxicated and feeling invincible. They waited in the parking lot for her to get off work.

It wasn't long before Casey exited the doors of her job. She worked during the day and went to Milwaukee Technical College at night. Her young life was filled with overtime at work and studying, until she met Jasso. Casey fell in love with him and moved in with him. Jasso paid all the bills so she could focus on school, but she kept her job because she did not want to be completely dependent on him. Casey smiled at the thought of being able to go home and spend the whole night with her man without having to rush out the door to make a class. She pulled out her phone and called Jasso to let him know she was on her way. The conversation did not last long because she knew he preferred to text, but she wanted to hear his voice.

As she made it to her car, Casey suddenly felt two powerful arms wrap around her and then lift her. She was then thrown into the backseat, and Boony slid beside her.

"Don't say shit, bitch, or I'll dead you right now!" Boony warned her as he tossed her car keys to Manace.

"Now, where do that man of yours live?"

He hit her on the top of her head with his fist to let her know he wasn't playing with her.

"Okay, okay! Please don't hit me anymore!" Casey pled with them before she gave them her address, praying Jasso still had his friends there with him that she heard in the background of their call.

Manace called Eshy, who followed close behind in the Impala.

"Cuz, ol' girl say this the house up here on the right."

"Okay. Y'all fall back. I'm going to ride passed and peep shit out before you pull in the driveway. Tell Boony to come hop in with me. You can handle that bitch, right?"

"Yeah, I got this here, cuz. Just do what you do!" he agreed, stopping Casey's car on the corner to let Boony out.

"Don't do shit until you see us on the side of the house!" Eshy ordered him.

When Boony was back in the Impala, Eshy slowly rode past the house. It didn't take much to realize that Casey had taken them to the right place. They spotted Jasso's van in the garage through its windows, so they quickly circled the block and rode by the house again before finding a parking space that would allow them an easy escape.

Inside the house, Jasso was hard at work breaking down and packing up kilos of coke to fill the orders that he had lined up. Zay proved to be more of an asset than he thought when they made that first trip. Zay not only shot first, but he also ran through kilos like a whore ran through rubbers.

Jasso was also liking the new Asad, now that he

was back on his feet. Asad not only pushed weed with Sky standing strongly at his side, but he also started moving cocaine like a pro. So adding the three of them to his team really got the product orders out for Jasso. When he heard a car pull up in the driveway, he looked up from the pot and out the side window. He saw it was Casey's Kia, so he didn't bother grabbing his gun that was lying on the counter when he went to let her in. As soon as Jasso turned the deadbolt, the door slammed into him and knocked him to the floor.

Eshy instructed Manace to send Casey in first just in case Jasso had a gun on him. Manace did as he was told, but to prove he was not afraid, he rushed through the door right behind her. Quick on his feet, Jasso dashed over and grabbed his gun and fired three shots. One of the shots hit Casey in her shoulder, which caused her legs to give out. But the other two bullets hit Manace in the chest. The young fool fell dead right on top of her.

After seeing his sixteen-year-old cousin hit the floor, Eshy rushed past Boony to his side. When he saw he was dead, Eshy shot Casey two more times and then emptied his clip into the house at Jasso, who by now had taken cover beside the stove. Jasso sent blind shots back at the door, just missing Boony's head by inches. Knowing the robbery was a bust, they turned and ran back to the car.

With her last bit of life, Casey picked up Manace's gun and sent a shot up Boony's back until she hit him in the head. But she didn't stop squeezing the trigger until the gun was empty. Sensing the gunfight was over, Jasso rushed over to her side.

"I'm sorry! I'm sorry! I love you!"

"No! Just hold on, baby! Casey, stay with me!" he pleaded.

"It's okay! I'm okay! It don't hurt no more."

She let out a low moan as blood began to spill from her mouth.

Jasso knew she was gone, so he quickly gathered up the money and drugs and stashed them in his van. Then he dialed 911 as he raced away from the house.

"I love you, Casey. I swear to God, I'm going to get them for you, baby!" he cried, looking in his rear-view mirror at the home he had made with her, one last time.

Chapter 14

Asad sat between China's legs on the floor in front of their leather sectional rolling a blunt and watching a movie with Jamie Foxx playing a kidnapped cab driver. Everything about him sitting like this with China felt familiar, and he wondered why, until he looked at a photo of him with his braids. China used to have him sit this way when she braided his hair. Asad could tell she missed that time by the way China was massaging his head.

The thing that happened with Sky had him doing whatever he could to avoid being alone with her. He let her handle his line for the night to keep her busy for as long as he could. She didn't mind, because she knew he was waiting on a call from Jasso, which Asad felt he should have gotten by now. He lit the blunt just as his phone rang Sky's ringtone.

"Sis, what it do? I was just thinking about you."

"I bet you was. But I'm done with that, and I got somebody I need you to meet. So what you got planned for the night?"

"Shit, I'm chilling with China right now though."

"Hey, girl! I know you need your time with him

too, so he's all yours. I got to go to work early tonight to break in the new girl," China told Sky as she handed the phone back to Asad, after grabbing it from him when she first heard Sky's voice.

She knew Asad was trying to get out of doing something, but thought he just wanted to be lazy.

"Let me find out if he's between your thighs while he's talking to me. Should I call back in two minutes?" Sky joked.

"She gave me the phone back. But you're right, I am between her legs right now."

"Don't say it like that, Asad. You making her think we doing something. Sky, he's just sitting on the floor!" China yelled in the background.

"Hey, I'm just telling it how it is. Now, how she takes it is on her," he laughed. "Who you want me to meet anyway?"

"This dude named Ron who I've been serving for a minute now. I met him through my sister. Anyways, he talking big, so I think you should have a sit-down with him to go over numbers," Sky explained.

"Okay, text me with the time and place. Make it public, and tell him to bring Tasha with him."

"What? You want to double date, bro? If you want to take me out, all you got to do is tell a bitch and I'm there!" Sky joked and then laughed at Asad's nervous silence.

"Whatever I want to do with you, you're going to be there ready and willing. Now text me and get off the phone."

He hung up on her before she could respond.

"Well, it was fun while it lasted!" China pouted playfully.

"I ain't gone yet. How much time do you got before you got to be at work?" he asked, sliding his hand up under one of his long shirts that she was wearing with nothing underneath.

"Enough for whatever you got on your mind!" China moaned as his fingers tickled her love button.

Asad pulled her to the edge of the sofa and then added his tongue to the party where he started between her thighs. His goal was to make her cum hard and fast while erasing the thoughts of making Sky do the same again. He didn't really want to go, but he needed the money she had for him for when he met up with Jasso when he called.

After taking a shower with China and making her cum harder than he had on the living room floor, Asad got out so she could get ready for work. He got dressed in a pair of icy-blue Trus, a crisp, white button-down, and Gucci loafers.

"Look at you all grown and sexy. If it was anybody else, your ass wouldn't be going nowhere without me!" China walked over and pulled out Asad's matching Rolex set. "Since you're dressing up, I think you should wear these."

"If you say so!"

He let her put the watch and bracelet on him, before he gave himself a once-over in the mirror. He and China then walked outside to their cars.

~ ~ ~

China called her sister and told her about Asad's idea for them to meet some place in public, thinking Ron would bring her to the meeting at the restaurant at which Sky had made reservations. She also thought it would be a good time to let Asad see her dress in her sexy clothes. As Sky sprinkled her bathwater with milk beads, she couldn't help but think of Penny. This would be the first time she went out to eat at a nice place without her.

Sky disrobed and climbed into the hot yet soothing water. She pressed play on the radio, turned up the volume, and then relit her blunt as soulful vocalist Kem sang one of Penny's favorite songs. His voice laced with Sky's thoughts of her lost love aroused her, and she didn't hold back. Sky let her imagination run away as her hand slid down her body.

Before long, tears rained down her face as she touched her breasts. She remembered how good it felt when Penny touched her this way. She flicked her fingers over her nipples, and then teased them by blowing on them the way her lover used to do. Her hand slipped further south down her flat abs until she reached her warmth. Sky danced her fingers around and in and out of herself until she felt a tugging feeling in her stomach she knew all too well.

"I love you, Penny. I love you!" Sky cried out as the first set of spasms came and released waves that took her breath away.

She wanted to feel something hard and thick inside of her, but she saved that itch for Asad to deal with later. Sky got out of the tub a few moments later and then dressed in the Dolce & Gabbana outfit she had picked out before her bath.

She then called her sister to give her a ride. She did not want to make it easy for Asad to avoid her. Sky knew he would not leave her stranded or make her take a cab home. A smile appeared on her face as she pinned up her locks.

"Hurry up, Skylar! I'm outside!"

"Where you at, Tasha? I don't see you, and I'm standing on the porch right now," she said, looking up and down the block for the car.

Right then a little red Saturn rounded the corner.

"Do you see me? Damn, sis! You look like you trying to take somebody's man or, I'm sorry, woman!" Tasha complimented Sky as she pulled over in front of her.

"Girl, stop! I'm just trying to get in where I fit in!"

Sky got in the car, hung up the phone, and said, "It ain't like that. But if China's with it, we can be one big happy family!"

"Yeah right, Sky! You know you don't want no dick in your life. And I know you're joking talking about bro like that. All this time we been knowing Asad. Never!"

Tasha looked over at Sky's big smile as they stopped for a group of UWM College kids to cross the street.

"Oh my goodness, Skylar! You serious right now. When this happen?"

"I don't know. I guess it's always been there!"

Tasha pulled back into traffic.

"Do this got anything to do with—?"

"No! Penny told me she knew how I felt about him long ago, and I just didn't see it until he got hurt."

"How do you think he's going to take knowing how you feel? What if this fucks up what you got going with him?"

"It won't fuck up nothing!" Sky assured her sister as they parked across from Ron's car.

"Okay! He's here!" Tasha said nervously as she checked herself in the rear-view mirror.

"Girl, you look good! Why you acting like this is

y'all's first date and shit?"

"Okay! I was going to wait and tell both of you in there, but I can't wait. Sky, you're going to be an auntie!"

"For real? Tasha, how far are you?" Sky asked excitedly while touching her sister's belly.

"I found out last week, but I didn't say nothing to nobody."

"Well let's get this show on the road. If shit don't go right tonight for us, we might be leaving the way we came."

They got out of the car and went inside to find the men already in a deep conversation at the table. The hostess called over a waiter to escort the sisters to the table. The waiter also took their drink orders and got refills for Asad and Ron.

"Wow is all I got to say to you in that dress!" Ron complimented Tasha when he saw her.

"Hey, you look fuckable tonight!" Asad whispered to Sky when she gave him a hug.

"You're joking, and I'm hoping!" she responded with a smile.

Before Asad could comment, his phone started vibrating. When he saw it was the caller he was waiting on, he excused himself from the table.

Chapter 15

To Jasso's relief, Amanda and the kids weren't home from a party at Monkey Joes they were invited to by one of their classmates. He bypassed the stairs leading to his bedroom and went right into his man cave that doubled as a spare bedroom when his in-laws came to visit. Right now, being locked away in the room was where he needed to be to clear his head before he had to face his wife and kids. Plus he needed to plan his next move.

The heartbroken hustler grabbed a bottle of Yukon Jack from the mini bar and then sat down in his favorite chair in front of the 150-gallon aquarium, where he usually enjoyed feeding helpless goldfish to the oscars while having a shot or two. But tonight, Jasso drank from the bottle as if it was the antidote to the pain in his heart. As he drank, he placed two calls—the first of which he had to try several times before Zay answered. When Zay picked up, Jasso told him about the attempted robbery and Casey's murder, and what he found out about the ones found dead at the scene. The next call was to Asad. He explained to him the same events that had taken place; only this time, he told Asad not to make a move until he heard back from him.

~ ~ ~

"Go get cleaned up and changed for bed," Amanda told the kids when she got them home.

Seeing her husband's van in its spot made her smile, but when she found the door to his den locked, she knew something was bothering him. Amanda let him alone for the time being, but she didn't plan on letting him push her away. Regardless of what was going on with Jasso, they were a team and would get through it together. After making sure their children were in bed, Amanda showered and prepared for bed herself.

"Jasso, baby! What you doing in there? Come to bed!" she called out to him from the other side of the locked door.

When she didn't get an answer, she put her ear to the door and heard him snoring.

Amanda went and got the key to the room and let herself in. He was fast asleep, just like she knew he would be. Amanda decided to get creative with waking him up. She undid his belt and pants since he had already kicked off his shoes. Seeing that Jasso's snoring remained even, she then pulled off his pants and boxers so she could easily get to what she wanted. Taking hold of Jasso's thickness, she licked and stroked it until it was fully erect. He was sound asleep, but his body reacted to her just the way she wished it would. Amanda planned to take full advantage of her husband.

Jasso mumbled Casey's name, but Amanda couldn't make it out and didn't let a phantom from his dream take the joy away from her.

"I guess we got ourselves a threesome!" Amanda joked. "But, bitch, I'm going first!"

She smiled and then buried his hardness in her mouth. She soon felt his hardness jerk in her mouth, alerting her that he was about to give her the drink for which she was working so hard.

That's when Jasso snapped awake and pushed her violently away from him, and then snatched his gun from the floor next to the chair.

"No, Jasso! Baby, it's me!" Amanda screamed, throwing her hands up in the air to get his attention.

"Fuck, Amanda! What the fuck! I could've killed you!" he said, dropping the gun and picking her up off the floor. "I'm sorry."

"No, no, baby! It's okay! I shouldn't have come in on you like this. Don't cry."

Somehow she sensed his tears were for more than what had just happened.

"Come on, Jasso. Let's go to our bed."

She took his hand, and he followed her upstairs

into their bedroom.

She finished undressing him and then helped him into bed.

"No, let me take a shower. I need to wash this drunk off of me."

Jasso stood up, staggered his way to the bathroom, and closed the door behind him.

"Do you want me to make you something to eat?" Amanda called behind him.

"No. I don't care!" he answered as he turned on the water in the shower and stepped inside, trying to let the hot water wash away the pain that fractured his heart.

Sometime in the middle of the night, Amanda woke up to Jasso screaming in his sleep.

"No, no! Don't die on me! Hold on! Please, just hold on!"

"Jasso! Jasso! Wake up." Amanda shook him, knowing he was reliving whatever had him in the mood she found him in earlier. "It's okay! You're at home now. It's just a dream," Amanda whispered while gently rubbing his chest.

He was awakened by his wife's caring touch. Panting with his body drenched in sweat, Jasso got out of bed and went into the bathroom. He splashed cold water on his face, trying to shake off the dream that had fresh tears streaming down his face. He then got himself together and went back to bed.

Chapter 16

It was a little after 8:00 a.m. when Zay made it safely back to Milwaukee. He had just spent the night sitting up in a lonely truck stop waiting for Miguel with Jasso's monthly shipment from Luis. Then he drove through the night, slapping himself a few times to stay awake and watching every set of headlights that got too close behind him.

Zay was now back home but beaten down by exhaustion from his journey through the state of Illinois. He could hardly stand up in the shower as he scrubbed away the smell of diesel and stale Black & Mild smoke that clung to him. The young thug thought of what Jasso told him, and he knew he needed to be at 100 percent to carry out the boss's orders when he woke up. Zay believed the punishment for murdering an innocent was death. It was the only true compensation for robbing one of his loved ones, and he planned on collecting the lives owed for taking Casey from Jasso and her family.

~ ~ ~

Everyone should know by now that the streets do talk, and they told Zay that he could find the ones he was hunting at Silks almost any night of the week. But it wasn't until the second night that Zay staked out the popular strip club that he caught sight of Freebandz in the car that Jasso had described to him.

Zay checked his watch. It was 9:45 p.m., yet it was still early enough for the parking lot to be open so he could sit and watch Freebandz and Summer fool around in the Impala. What he didn't know was that she was a player in a lot of Freebandz's robberies. Zay eased out of the backseat of the gray Chevy TrailBlazer that he had stolen earlier that day, and made his way over to his target.

The two were so caught up in their quickie that neither of them noticed the messenger of death standing right outside the window. Just as Freebandz was about to release his load down Summer's throat, Zay snatched the door open and savagely rained a blow down on his victim's face, breaking his nose along with a few teeth. Zay then clamped an arm around Freebandz's neck and attempted to pull him out of the seat. Freebandz fought to keep his consciousness as he struggled with his attacker. He tried desperately to reach his gun under the driver's seat as the hold continued to tighten around his neck. He felt a sense of hope when his fingers closed around the Glock 23.

Summer snapped out of her shock and snatched up the gun.

"Let him go!"

"Fuck you, bitch!" Zay said as he pulled Freebandz out of the car.

Summer saw this and started shooting wildly at him. Zay quickly dropped behind the back door. He pulled out his second gun and sent shots into the body of Freebandz, while firing a few at Summer before he made his getaway. Zay heard the stripper let out a scream that told him his job was well done. Once he was safely back inside the SUV, he promised not to play with the next one, so he went to swap back into his own car that he had parked not far from the club.

Knowing the police would be there soon, Summer ran from the car still holding the gun in her hand as she put as much distance between her and Freebandz's body as she could. Summer did have sense enough to grab her knock-off Jimmy Choo bag which held her phone. She called Cash while slowing her wild run to a fast walk.

"I thought you had to work?" he answered.

"Come get me right now! I'm outside of the Mobile gas station on 91st and Silver Spring!" Summer yelled into the phone.

"Wait, what's up? What's wrong?"

"I don't want to say on the phone. Just please come get me!"

Summer was shaking, crying, and jumpy, not knowing if she had been followed or why the shooting had happened.

"Summer, I'm already on my way."

Cash swung his car around doing almost 60 mph on the city street as he headed back north on 76th Street.

"I'll call you when I get up there."

"No! Stay on the phone with me. I don't know if he's going to come back for me not."

"Summer, what are you talking about?" Cash asked, slowing down when he reached Silver Spring to let police cars heading in the same direction jet by him.

He followed right behind them blowing through stoplights and all.

"I'll tell you when you get here. I can't say on the phone."

Cash pulled into the gas station.

"I'm here! Where you at?"

"I'm across the street by the post office!" Summer said as she stood up from sitting on the curb. "I see you. Can you see me?" she asked, jumping up and down while waving her arms.

Cash quickly skipped across the busy street to her.

"Is that blood on you?"

He pulled off before she had the door closed.

"Free's dead!"

"What!"

He looked at her in shock.

"Bitch! What you do?" Cash demanded to know as he pulled the car to a stop on the side of the street.

"I didn't do it! I didn't do nothing! We was outside the club, when out of nowhere, this dude jumped in the car and grabbed him. I tried to help. I took the gun and shot at him, but he was too fast, and he started shooting back. I got scared and ran!"

"Bitch! Who was it?"

He pulled his gun out to let her know he wasn't playing with her.

"Cash, I don't know for real." She shielded her face in case he decided to hit her. "On my kids' lives, I didn't have shit to do with it."

"So, y'all was just sitting in the parking lot when this happened?" he asked as he turned around and began heading back that way.

"Yeah! We was in the parking lot, and I was sucking his dick. Is that what you want to know?"

"Look, Summer, you know I know how you get down. I just need to know what I'm walking into. What did you do with the gun?"

"I got it in my purse."

She pulled it out for him to see.

"Give it here!"

Cash took it and put it in his stash spot under the

dashboard along with his, because the police were all over the place. Cash drove in close enough to see Freebandz slumped halfway over in the car.

"Yeah, it's over for folks."

"I know. Let's just get away from around here before they see me. Everybody knows he's my baby daddy. I know one of them bitches told the police that I was here and shit."

"You good for now, but I think you should get home and call the police and tell them what happened. Just leave out the part about you shooting back at them when you do."

"What? I'm not doing that. What if they ask me why I didn't call them right away? Then what?"

"You lost your phone, and when you saw me, you flagged me down and I took you home." Cash explained as he headed to her project. "Summer, I got you. I'm going to stay with you until it's over."

~ ~ ~

At the far end of Silks' parking lot, Zay sat in his dark tan and gold 2009 Dodge Charger sitting on 23" forged rims with the thick and sexy stripper that told them Freebandz would be at the strip club tonight.

"You riding with me, or you staying here to answer questions?"

He already knew she was coming with him,

because she wanted the rest of the money Asad had promised her for the information.

"No, boo! I don't talk to no police. They might have some shit on my ass for all I know."

"I want to put something on that ass, if you going?" he said, eyeing her big legs that sparkled from the shimmer body lotion she had on for her stage show that was cut short because of the murder.

"If you can do something with lil' daddy, then yeah. But if you can't handle it, you can just take a bitch to the crib."

Forever flirted with Zay, but she had no idea she was face to face with death in the flesh.

"I can show you better!" he told her as she got out of the car and then went back into the club to get her things. "Why not smash that sexy ass before I kill it, you bitch! When you dead, you can't run your mouth to nobody," he said out loud to no one.

He then looked out the window and saw the police trying to make sense of what the murder was about.

When Forever got back into the car, Zay pulled off and headed to the nearest and cheapest motel he could find.

Chapter 17

All Eshy knew was that Forever had told one of the other girls at Silks that she was going on a date with a guy named Zack, before she was found dead in a motel by its cleaning staff. The girl also gave them the photo of the car and its plate number that she had taken a picture of in case Forever didn't make it back from the date. But the girl didn't turn over the information she had to the police. When she called Summer to ask her what she should do, because she didn't want to be a witness in the case, Summer told her that she would take care of it. That's when a dancer named ShyAnn gave her a description of the guy who was behind the wheel of the car in the photo.

Summer knew the guy ShyAnn had described to her was the same guy who killed Freebandz, and she told Eshy. Now he knew that the car belonged to a Latin King named Zay, not Zack, and that he could be found on the south side at Lincoln Park for a unity basketball game between the Kings and the Lords on the weekend. Eshy made plans to get revenge for his friends.

~ ~ ~

Asad and China had just pulled away from the park on their way to pick up some more weed for the celebration, when two unknown cars pulled up outside of the fenced-in basketball courts.

"We didn't come over here to play with these bitch-ass niggas. Drop everything, move on court, and get the fuck out of here!" Eshy reminded his guys, before getting out of the car and letting his AK spray the unsuspecting ballplayers.

The rest of the men he led followed suit, sending hot slugs up and down the courts.

The Kings and Lords did not know what hit them, but that didn't stop them from returning fire as pandemonium broke out all around the park. Many civilians were dropping to the ground from getting shot and slipping as they ran to get out of the way of the gunfire.

Jasso was talking to Amanda, who was helping with the food before the shooting started. He pushed his wife to the ground and ran to get to his gun to return fire once he saw his children were safe in the recreational building. The Lords and Kings continued to return fire even though their Glocks were no match for the rapid fire of the big AK-47s.

Zay took cover behind a tree as he shot back at the carloads of assassins. When his gun was empty, he ran zig-zagging his way through the park while trying to make it to his car for his other gun. Slugs whizzed by Zay so close that one ripped through his hoody. He looked over his shoulder just in time to see one of the two men stalking across the grass turn his gun his way. Zay dove to the ground and was helplessly pinned there until one of his vice Lord brothers drove his truck straight at the gunmen, drawing all of their fire on him while attempting to buy time for his people to get clear.

Eshy saw Zay get up from the ground, and he went after him shooting as he gave chase. One of Milwaukee's finest tried to hit Eshy with his cruiser, but the revenge-crazed thug sent shots through the cop's windshield and let his true target get away.

"Fam, get the fuck in the car!" one of Eshy's men yelled at him, stopping not too far from him. "It's over, E. Let's go, man!"

After seeing all the police and SWAT vehicles flood the park, Eshy did as he was told and escaped to see another day.

Zay made it to his car and quickly stormed off, only slowing to pick up a few of his guys before leaving the area.

Jasso ran as hard as he could with the police hot on his tail. He cut through a yard, blindly ran across the alley, and hopped a gate to the yard on the other side. The homeowner's big pit bull did his job and chased Jasso over the front gate, until his master called him home.

"Jasso! Jasso!" China called to her friend as he rounded the car.

"Bro, get your slow ass in the car!" Asad ordered. Hearing his name being called and seeing Asad's red Infinity Q50 appear was all the encouragement Jasso needed to stop running and get in the car.

"Go! Get the fuck out of here!"

Asad pulled into traffic nice and easy.

"Chill out, bro! You good now. Here! You better call Mandy. She's worried sick about you. She called me and told me that you were being chased this way. That's how I knew where to look for you!" he explained as he tossed Jasso his phone to make a call to his wife.

"Okay. She'll have to wait until I catch my breath."

"I ain't gonna lie. I thought the dog was going to get you. I bet if the police wasn't on that ass, he would have caught you!" China teased him.

"Damn! Was you really cheering for the dog?" Jasso laughed as he dialed Amanda's phone number.

~ ~ ~

The police pulled over the car that Eshy was in, just before it crossed the 16th Street viaduct.

"What are you in such a hurry for?" the cop asked

the driver, Tony.

"I'm sorry, sir. My nerves are still fucked up. My girl just called and told me that my son got hit by a car, and I'm trying to get to the hospital," Eshy explained, once he saw how nervous Tony was.

"Don't tell me they were at Lincoln?" the officer asked, after having heard about the shoot-out in the park and all of the accidents because of it.

"I don't know where they was at. I'm just trying to get to the hospital to be with my baby."

"Go ahead and get there, but slow it down. It ain't good for nobody if you all end up in the hospital with him."

"Alright. Thank you, sir," Tony said after he was able to breathe again as the officer let him go with a warning.

He pulled off at the posted speed limit.

"Man, fam! I thought I was going to have to have court in the street. Because I ain't going back to the joint without a fight."

"Get the fuck outta here with that tough shit. You was shaking and shit!" one of the other two men in the car teased.

"Yeah, because I was getting ready to pop his ass!" Tony told him, before he showed him the gun he had hidden under his leg.

Eshy put his head back on the seat. He was still mad that Zay got away from him. He was already trying to think of how to catch up to Zay again, and he wondered if he had seen Jasso in the middle of all the havoc. If so, he would make him pay for Freebandz's murder along with his little flunky.

"Drop me off at the liquor store in the hood. I'll walk to the house."

"Okay, E. I'll let ya out when we get to the spot?"

"Yeah, my nig! Y'all just get there and do something with these guns, and find out who all made it okay. I just need to clear my head and plan our next move," Eshy told his men.

Chapter 18

A little short of ninety days after the shoot-out at the park, it was back to business as usual as $1.2 million breezed through the streets chauffeured by Jasso in his wife's champagne-pink Audi TT convertible. He was on his way to Timber Field Airport to hand the money over to Roberto.

Roberto was Luis's younger brother and his personal pilot. Arriving right on time, Jasso found him doing the pre-flight check of the plane.

"Hey, man, you missed a spot right over there."

"You're always on time, my friend." Roberto looked up from his list but didn't stop his inspection. "It's what I like about you, Jasso. You always get me in and out, unlike a lot of the jokers I got to pick up from."

"Well, all our time is money, and for the love of money, I don't waste time. Speaking of time, I'm going to go ahead and put these inside the plane for you."

Jasso placed the three duffel bags of small bills inside the cab of the plane.

"Brother, one of my trips you're going to have to

show me your city. This is the only place I've been where I haven't sampled a taste of the sweet pussies."

They both laughed as Roberto strapped himself into the pilot's seat.

"Have a safe one!" Jasso bid the pilot as the powerful twin engines roared to life.

"You too, my friend."

As the plane taxied down the runway, Jasso sat in the Audi on the phone with Luis.

"It's on its way to you right now," he said as Roberto lifted off smoothly into the air.

"So, all is well, I take it?"

"You should know by now that it always is, but I'll be coming to see you soon. We need to sit down and talk about the future."

"My friend, you're always welcome to come sit down with me," Luis told him, before they ended the call.

The Audi pulled back out onto Appleton Avenue and headed for the expressway. Jasso was heading home. During the drive he recalled the conversation he had with Amanda after Casey's death.

"I can't take what you're doing to yourself, Jasso. I can't take what you're doing to our family. You're always away from us. Even when you're here in this house, it's like you're not with us."

Jasso remembered her tears.

"Fuck the money! Fuck everything. I just want

my husband back. Don't you know all we need is you, Jasso?"

He had done very well for himself in the drug game, and he knew it wasn't going to last forever. He turned onto the off ramp and stopped at a red light. He then thought of Casey and once again asked God why she had to die.

"Yes, it's time for me to get out of this shit and let someone else take it over," he said out loud to himself.

A few moments passed before his phone starting vibrating. He passed a slow driver before he answered.

"What up, bro?"

"Shit! Shit! Just calling to tell you I got everything handled that you needed me to, and I made sure to clean up afterward," Zay told him, referring to the latest hits that Jasso put out.

Hearing about the murders put a smile on his face for the first time in months. "Thank you! That's just the news I needed to get from you." Jasso pulled to stop at another light. "Bro, can you meet up with me later round 11:30?"

"Yep, I don't got shit else to do tonight."

"Okay, and call Asad for me and tell him I want to see him too. Y'all can pick the spot as long as it's somewhere I can get a drink."

"Okay then, bro! It's ladies' night at Zarkos, and

unlike you two, I don't have no in-house pussy waiting on me when I walk through the door," he joked as he texted Asad.

Asad texted back, "No! Let's meet up at the Rave. Byrd's having his birthday party there, and it's going to be packed."

~ ~ ~

Ron shook his head in frustration with his kids' mother because she found out about Tasha from one of her friends who worked at the Planned Parenthood at which Tasha walked in to get help.

"You know you're still fucking that bitch, Ronnie. If you wasn't, then why you trying to make her get rid of her baby? Bitch-ass nigga, answer that!"

Without thinking, he punched his wife, Melissa, in the face and knocked her to the floor.

"Bitch! Watch your mouth, and don't worry about what I do as long as you and this house are good. So shut the fuck up with all that shit, bitch, before I really fuck you up!"

Melissa picked herself up off the floor and walked over to the small bar where she had hidden one of his guns for the next time he decided to put his hands on her.

"Fuck you! You ain't right! You ain't right!" she

kept repeating.

"What, bitch? I'll show you me not being right!"

He stalked up behind her about to hit her again, when she suddenly turned around with the gun aimed at him.

"Put—put that gun down before somebody gets hurt, Lissa!" he said while slowly backing away yet keeping his eyes on the gun shaking in her hands.

"Oh, now you're worried about somebody getting hurt, punk!" she screamed and then spit blood from her busted lip. "Don't you think it just hurt me when you hit me in my face, Ronnie?" The gun shook harder. "Don't you think it hurt when that little bitch walked up on my friends and told them she was having your baby?" Melissa was crying, but suddenly just stopped and starred at him for several moments. "Get out!" she said in a soft shaky voice. "Get the fuck out of my house!" she snapped.

"Baby, this is our house!"

"Punk, don't call me that. Bitch, just get the fuck out!"

Ron decided to try her and took two steps toward her, and Melissa shot at his feet.

"Oh shit!"

He jumped back and froze, praying she wouldn't shoot him the next time she pulled the trigger.

"Get the fuck out before I kill your punk ass up in this bitch."

Melissa raised the gun until it was pointing at his chest.

Ron didn't try her again. He just did what he was told and slowly backed out of the house. Once he was outside, he made a dash to his car and stormed off. Before he turned the corner, Melissa was blowing up his phone.

"What?" he answered.

"So, Ronnie, you just going to leave us?" she asked crying. "Where you going? To your little bitch's house? I bet that broke bitch still stays at home with her mama."

"Fuck you, Lissa! Bitch, you crazy as hell! Did you forget you just told me to get out?" He turned onto Capital Drive. "Stupid bitch, you shot at me! Bitch, get the fuck off my line!" he snapped, before he hung up on her.

He wiped away his own tears. He was mad at himself for hitting her when she had every right to be upset. Melissa called back several times before he answered.

"Stop calling me, Lissa."

"No, not until you talk to me, Ronnie. I'm sorry! I shouldn't have shot at you, but you promised you wouldn't hit me again and you did."

"Lissa, you're right! I'm the one that needs to be apologizing to you, but right now you just got to stop calling me so I can get my mind right. Let's just chill for now."

"Baby, you know I don't want it to be over with us. Me and the kids need you."

"Let's just talk in the morning or something."

"So you're not coming to the house tonight? Fuck you, bitch! I just wanted—!"

Ron hung up on her again and then turned up Yo Gotti's song "Touch Down" and let the deep bass from his four 12" subwoofers drown out Melissa's back-to-back calls. Ron raced his Pepsi-painted, 1985 two-door Chevy Nova sitting on 24" razor rims down Capital.

He decided to get off the streets just in case she called the police and told them about the gun he always kept in the car. Ron pulled up and parked across from an ABC Plumbing box truck and walked into one of his most profitable drug houses, without giving the work truck any thought.

Ron was the head of a small clique known as Certified Hamp Boyz, and right now they were inside the house on 19th and Hampton having a good old time drinking, partying, and selling drugs like it was legal. The sounds of Lil Phat, one of the clique's favorite rappers, shook the walls of the house and could be heard down the block.

Ron wouldn't usually allow this, but he didn't care tonight. He just grabbed a bottle of beer and joined in. One of his foolish youngsters carelessly sold to an undercover cop not once but more than six times, with the unfamiliar bi-racial couple buying larger amounts than they did each time before, knowing the foolish teen was in a hurry to get back to the party.

Soon Ron was high and a bit drunk, so he plucked one of the females from the party. He then took her into one of the bedrooms to release the stress of the fight with Melissa deep into her warmth.

~ ~ ~

"We just got the warrant. It's a go with the bust," the eager drug taskforce detective announced to his team.

The MPD drug taskforce was stationed in back of the plumbing truck, and on the opposite end of the block were two unmarked cars helped with surveillance. The team geared up to storm the one-story house.

"Let's be careful going in. Remember, there are civilians inside with these punks. So don't shoot if you don't have to, and for the love of God, don't shoot one of them," the detective ordered before he led them into the house.

At almost 11:30 p.m. the nervous but skilled SWAT team took their places in the front and rear of the house. On the detective's mark, the men simultaneously broke in the doors. From the rear door, an officer shot a pit bull that was chained next to the kitchen door. The team that came through the front found Ron in a bedroom just off the living room asleep in the arms of a seventeen-year-old female. They also found three fully automatic guns, over two hundred grams of crack, and a loaded Glock in the pocket of Ron's jacket with his driver's license. Sadly, the police knew Asad's name before they had both of Ron's hands cuffed.

Chapter 19

Byrd's party was an open invite, and everyone who was anyone came out to have a good time and show love. Station V-100.7 sent out the invitations every hour on the hour all week long. This brought out not only the ballers but also the wannabes, but everyone came dressed to impress. Byrd had the entire VIP area closed off for only his family and friends. His sisters put it all together for him and did all the cooking for the VIP area, but his oldest sister, Felisha, hired caterers to feed the rest of the hall.

When Asad walked through the doors to the ballroom with China and Sky, they were ambushed by servers with drinks and the hot sounds of Miltown's number-one party deejay, Homer Blow, doing his thing, mixing and matching the new and old-school hits the way he did best. Zay spotted the trio not far from the entrance and sent the sexy waitress he was flirting with to get them, but not before he stored her phone number in his phone.

On the way to the table in the VIP area, they detoured to wish Byrd a happy and blessed birthday. When they made it over to him, he was being pulled up onto the small stage by four of the hottest female strippers in the city. ShyAnn, Suckcess, and Kandi Girl gave Byrd a lap dance to remember, while Nuda Angel danced around and collected the tips that were being rained onto the stage. As 50 Cent's "In Da Club" pounded out from the speakers, Nuda Angel and Kandi Girl put on their signature girl-on-girl show at Byrd's feet for him and the crowd. The dancers were Sky and Asad's gift to him along with a card that China handpicked containing $1,000 in cash.

"Hey, my divas! I'm glad y'all slow asses finally got here. Now let's go to the bathroom so these guys can talk. I can't hold it no more, so let's go!" Amanda said, leading the way from VIP to the restrooms with Sky and China in tow.

"So what up, bro-bro?" Asad asked, not wasting time beating around the bush.

Both he and Zay wanted to know the reason Jasso had called them together.

"It's like this. I feel like I had my run in this game."

He paused, looking them both in the face, trying to judge their reaction to what he was saying to them.

"Man, bro! What you saying for real?" Zay asked.

"It's time for me to get out of these streets. Don't say shit yet. Just hear me out!" Jasso told them so they wouldn't cut him off again. "I got my cash way up. I don't have to worry about shit. The car lots are doing good, and y'all know how me and my cousin's club do numbers every time the doors open. My kids and Mandy need me home more now. I've been hustling so hard in these streets that I really don't know my kids the way I should. I don't want them to ever feel the way I do about my pops, so I'm done."

Asad dropped his head at the thought of his friend getting out of the game. He never thought he would ever hear these words from Jasso, especially when the money was coming in the way it was. Before he could ask Jasso the big question, Zay spoke up.

"So, bro, where do that leave us?"

"Well, I already set up shit with Luis. He's looking forward to continuing things with the two of you. The next step is yours."

"How would that work?" Zay asked, taking the words right out of Asad's mouth.

"It's all the same, but just without me. You'll still go meet our guy every month for the drop. Asad, you will take over for me and meet Roberto for the pickup. I think splitting the line up between the two of you will keep things on the up-and-up, but I got one better. I'm going to give it to Sky and Asad. You can handle all my people on my line because you're more of a level-headed type of person than she is. And before you say anything, I already talked to her about it. I just didn't tell her that I was getting out, and I told her not to say shit until I had more time to think."

Jasso took a sip of his drink and then asked both of them how they felt about what he had decided.

"What the fuck? There's something going on over there. Look!" Zay announced, after noticing many of the partygoers rushing back into the hall.

Asad and Jasso stood to get a better view.

"Which way did the girls go to the bathroom?" Asad asked them while pushing his way toward the disturbance.

~ ~ ~

Summer arrived with Eshy and Cash, and they were all dressed to impress. They were met by the newest members of Eshy's robbery crew: Dannyboy, Von, Punch, and Southside. Southside was the brother of ShyAnn, the stripper who was riding Byrd's lad onstage.

A few females who Summer knew from her dancing days pulled her away from Cash. She and Cash started messing around behind Freebandz's back when he was living, but now that he was gone, they were letting it show.

After showing off her unique skills on the dance floor, Summer and her friends made their way to the ladies' room to freshen up. A mixture of smoke and perfume filled the air of the spacious and very clean restroom. Only two women besides Amanda, Sky, and China were in there when Summer and her friends walked in.

"Sky! Sky!" China tapped her on the leg excitedly, but trying not to draw attention to them.

"Bitch, stop hitting me! I'm right here. What up?" Sky asked, passing the peach-flavored blunt to Amanda.

"What I miss?" Amanda asked, not taking her eyes off the women she noticed China getting excited about as she hit the weed.

"That's the hoe that got Asad jumped at All Stars!" China said as she took off her heels.

"China, are you sure?" Sky asked, feeling her anger growing at the memory of Asad lying helpless in the hospital.

"Yeah, Sky. I was right there. I'll never forget that bitch. She got away that night, but she won't tonight."

"Fuck yeah! Let's beat that ass. I ain't beat a hoe up since my high school days!" Amanda told them, almost sounding excited to fight.

China walked over to block Summer's path to the mirrors, and a small spark of recognition cracked her face before Sky's right cross crashed into Summer's jaw. One of her friends moved to help, but Amanda sent her face-first into the hand dryer, by grabbing the woman by her hair and swinging her away from China. The others ran out to tell someone what was going down in the restroom.

Summer did not have a chance with the two enraged women. Once she hit the floor, it was over for her. They gave her the same stomping that Asad had received because of her. Amanda continued to bang her victim's head against the wall until she was bleeding and knocked out cold. Amanda then joined her friends in the merciless beating they were putting on poor, helpless Summer. Soon the Rave's security team rushed in to pull the women off of her.

~ ~ ~

Armed with two bottles of champagne taken from the birthday party, the three friends laced adrenalin with liquor as they danced around Sky's living room while still explaining and acting out the fight that got them kicked out.

"Bae, how did you know it was the same bitch that got me jumped? I looked at what was left of them on our way out, and I can't remember neither of them," Asad asked as he got up from the plush La-Z-Boy and stood between Sky and China.

"Asad, really? Nigga, you can hardly remember how to get home half of the fucking time!" Sky teased.

"Hey, bitch, don't do my baby!" China defended him before they all laughed. "But really, Asad! I'd know that funny-faced hoe from any muthafucking where with her ugly ass."

"Well, the bitch wasn't all that ugly before we got a hold of her, but I'm sure she is now!" Sky joked, laughing at her own comment.

"Sky, don't make me fuck you up. I'm the baddest bitch!" China then took off her dress right in front of them.

"Yeah, you right!" Sky agreed as she pulled China over and kissed her.

Seeing this act both shocked and aroused Asad. Giving into lust, China pulled him in to join the kiss. Sky undid his belt while China pulled off his shirt. After that, garments were being tossed wherever they fell as the trio made their way to Sky's queen-sized bed. Asad lay back on the bed to enjoy the show and wondered if this was the first time they had done this.

China nervously looked into Sky's eyes to let them tell her this was her first time being with another woman. Sky cupped China's face and kissed her again with such passion, she knew she wasn't going to stop what was started. Sky broke the kiss by roughly pushing China down on top of Asad, who quickly covered China's lips with his own.

"I love you so much, Asad," China said.

"I love you too," he responded as Sky took his hardness deep in her mouth.

He then pulled China up and began sucking on her hard nipples.

China let him play with her breasts until she couldn't take Sky having all the fun teasing him with her lips. China dropped down and took over sucking and licking her man. Sky made her way up his chest to his lips.

"I love you too," he told her while looking deep into her eyes.

"I know you do," Sky answered, smiling hard.

She had been waiting for this moment all night, and China was a welcomed bonus.

He pushed Sky off of him onto her back and then pulled China up and did the same. Asad pushed her closer to Sky, and Sky pulled her over her face to get a taste of her wetness. Asad moved between Sky's thick legs, where he began fingering her wetness before lifting her legs over his shoulders and burying his thickness inside of her.

"Oh yes! Oh yes!" the women moaned in pure pleasure.

Sky skillfully manipulated Asad's moves, thrusting her hips up to meet his strokes. China arched her back from the pain of Sky's nail digging in her butt and the pleasure of her skillful tongue. Before she drowned Sky with her juices, China climbed off her face; and after soaking Asad with hers, Sky pulled him up on the bed where she took him in her mouth again. She felt his hardness swell again and pulled China over it. She happily straddled him, forcing herself down on his thickness. Sky sucked and kissed on his neck, jaw, and lips. When Asad came for the second time deep inside China, they all collapsed.

Asad held them tightly in his arms feeling an authority that he never felt before. He kissed the top of their heads and fell asleep.

Chapter 20

In the heart of First District in downtown, Ron sat in a cold lonely interrogation room waiting for someone to come talk to him. He had been in the room for hours before the two detectives walked into the room and woke him up.

"What's up, buddy? I'm Detective Mavric, and this is Detective Moore. Is there anything you need before we get started?"

"And before you ask, I'm sorry, but they don't let us allow you to smoke in here anymore," Moore told Ron.

"But, hell, if the info you were so eager to share when you got picked up is as good as I think it is, then I don't see why we couldn't bend that rule for you!" Mavric said with a sneaky smile.

"What do I get for what I got to say?"

"Well, that depends on how far you're willing to work with us. If you go undercover, I believe that can get you out the door with a slap on the hand."

"Yeah, probation is much, much better than prison for—!" Moore began, before he took a glance at the notepad he was holding, "—the fifteen to twenty-five years you're facing with us just on the gun and drugs. But then if you factor in the under-age girl you were caught with in bed, you can add on maybe another five years."

"Now that five will be what gets you, because them boys in the big house don't respect no one with under-age sex cases!" Mavric added.

"Hey, I don't get down like that. I didn't know how old she was. The bitch told me she was old enough!" Ron explained to them.

"Look, Ron, I don't give a fuck about some little hood rat getting fucked by you. All I care about is drugs. If you give us what we need, I'll make that part of the case go away. But if you play with me, I'll make sure they put you in the cell with the biggest son of a bitch I can find and tell him you like them young."

That was all Ron needed to hear for him to tell them all they needed to know about his dealings with Asad. However, he left out all the parts about Sky, thinking that if he told them about her, it would be easy for Asad to pinpoint who talked.

"So, will you go in wired up to make a buy for us?" Mavric asked.

"Yeah, I will. But how you going to explain me getting out of here? The streets talk, and I know the whole hood knows by now that I'm in here."

"Well, I'm sure you can come up with a good

excuse on your own!" Mavric told him.

Moore could see that Ron was thinking of backing out of their deal.

"How about we set bail for you at a price you will need a little help paying?" he suggested. "This way, you can maybe get your guy on the phone when you ask him for help paying the bail?"

"Okay, I can do that. But I want my money back. I'm going to need it to fall back on if he ever finds out it was me that set him up," Ron told them, trying his best to make Asad look like a real kingpin to them.

The detectives agreed and then left to put things in motion. They sent an officer to take Ron to booking an hour later. They had to take him through the whole intake process to make the arrest look credible. The booking room officers had to move Ron to a housing unit because of the overcrowding of the holding cells. They promised him that as soon as things went through, he would be back out on the streets.

When Ron made it through the night on the cell block, he rushed to the phones as soon as the dayroom was open the next morning. It had been two days since he talked to Melissa. He prayed she would answer the phone when he called, and he hated all that had happened to him at the same time they had their fight.

"Hello? Ron, what happened? Where you at? I've been calling the county for you," she answered.

"Lissa, we only got a sec on this call. Put money on the phone so I can call back, and I'll explain. I— I!"

The free call was disconnected before he could tell Melissa he loved her. He called Tasha and repeated the process of telling her to set up the phone so he could call her. The only difference was that he was able to tell her that he loved her, but he was only softening Tasha up because he would need her to put out the word that he needed bail money. He knew she would ask Sky for the money, and Sky would then tell Asad. Then he could get out and get this mess with the detectives over with.

Ron walked away from the phones taking in his surroundings while trying to find a familiar face in the dayroom. When he couldn't find one, he went back into his cell to wait for Melissa and Tasha to get the phone lines unblocked.

~ ~ ~

"Skylar, what do you think I should do?"

"T, you know I say fuck him! Let the punk wifey pooh get him out, but I know you're not going to do that."

"No, I'm not. He's still my baby daddy, and I still

129

love him, sis," Tasha admitted to Sky while rubbing her big belly after the baby kicked.

"I'll take care of it. I got you, girl. But that love shit you talking is just the baby talking. You know that fool-ass nigga ain't going to leave his bitch for real."

Sky lit up the blunt she had finished rolling.

"Did he say what he got caught with or anything like that?"

"Nope! He just said they ran up in the house, and he needed to get out so he could get him and his guys a lawyer."

"I'll get it done for you. Tell the fool I said he better have all mine when his ass touches these bricks, because I ain't going to play with him. He's your BD, not mine!"

"Sky, stop!"

"How much is the bail?" Sky asked.

Tasha told her he did not know yet, but as soon as he found out he'd call her.

"I'll have my people look into it," Sky told her before she ended the call.

She told Jasso, and he put his connections to work for her.

Chapter 21

Six had been doing time in the dirty county jail for a little over two months on a fourteen-day probation hold by the time Ron made it onto the pod. Six had heard about the raid within hours of it, because his little sister was one of the young girls in the house when the police kicked in the doors. He was cool with Byrd and knew that Ron dealt with Asad, who was one of Byrd's Lord brothers, so he called Byrd.

"Bro-bro, did you know your guy Ron is in the county? I got one of my niggas in that bitch on a PO hold in the pod with him."

"Yeah, I just found out the dude got bitch in him. He ain't right, feel me? Big bro got a tag on him, so if your guy can make that happen for us, we will make sure he's good."

"Say no more, homie. I'm on it!" Byrd assured Asad. "You can just deal with me. As soon as I'm out and about, I'll hit you up so we can talk more. Now if you ain't sure, let me know now, because when I say go, it's too late."

"Better safe than sorry. No witness, no case—remember?" Asad told Byrd.

The two of them made small talk about the Bucks game and cars before they ended their conversation.

~ ~ ~

After the evening meal, Ron made his way to the officer's desk to have his bracelet scanned for the third time that day. He still did not have bail set, and he was starting to think the detectives had played him.

"Okay, what would you like to know?" the CO asked after looking up from his screen.

"Do I got a bail yet? This shit's crazy. I should've been out of this bitch a long time ago!" Ron answered in frustration.

"Well, if you don't break the law, you don't have to ever be in this bitch. But your bail is $35,000, so it looks like you're going to be here for awhile unless you have a rich uncle someplace," the officer joked.

"You got me fucked up like I'm one of these other fools. You better look at what I'm here for. My bitch got that shit in her purse," Ron boasted before he then rushed over to the phones.

"Hey, fam, let me get that after you," he said to the guys on the phones.

"Cross, come to the desk!" Ron heard the officer call his last name.

He walked over thinking his bail was paid

already, knowing that Melissa had access to his money.

"Yeah, tell me something good."

"You have a professional visit out in the hall. Is that good enough for Mr. Baller?"

Ron walked off the dorm floor and found Detective Moore waiting for him.

"Ron, how you holding up?" he asked, once they were behind closed doors in the interview room.

"Good, now that the bail is set. What took so long?"

"That's part of why I'm here. My partner is over at the DA's office as we speak trying to get him to sign off on the deal. Wait! Did you say you have a bail now?"

"Yeah, it's thirty-five bands."

"Okay then, that means it's a go for us! Can you hold off on getting the bail paid until say noon tomorrow? It's a little late to spring this on my team right now when we've had a busy and long day already?"

"I don't know. My girl might already be down here. I was about to call her when you pulled me out here."

"If so, I'm just going to have to put a hold on you until then. Do you really think she came up with that type of money that fast? If so I'm going to be happy to get this Asad King off the streets. Anyone who can throw that kind of cash away just like that is dangerous."

"That's why you can't let what I'm doing get out. I got kids, and I don't want nothing to happen to them or my girl."

What Ron really didn't want was for it to get out and damage his street credibility, so he could remain on top in his crew.

"Don't worry about that. You just try to hold off paying the bail, and leave King to me," Moore told him, before he sent him back to the dorm.

~ ~ ~

Back in the dayroom of the jail, Six was sitting at a table with a wild youngster who had just gotten sentenced to life plus fifty years, as if life wasn't enough.

"There he goes. Right there at the door!"

"Oh yeah, I know him from over there on Hampton. I was thinking of robbing him, but my uncle wouldn't let me. I knew I didn't like him for a reason."

"Well, handle your business, and then ten rakes will be put on your books by the morning or however you want it."

"Ten rakes? Yeah, a nigga need that where I'm going, to get a TV and a radio and shit when I get to the joint," the youngster explained, already spending the money in his mind. "But can you have your people give it to my sister? I don't want these white folks to take it before I get up there. They gave me all kinds of fines and shit."

"I'll have them take her half tonight just to show you it's good. And, homie, I'll make sure the fellas got your back up there so you won't be alone!" Six promised him.

When the youngster agreed, Six walked him to the phone to call his girl, and had her call the kid's sister on a three-way line. Six then told his girl to take the kid's sister $5,000. He passed the phone to the kid so he could talk to his sister.

"I got you, Larry. But what you doing for this?"

"Sis, I told you I got muthafuckas that love me in the Mill. You just don't let nobody know you got that, and you can keep two rakes for yourself. You all I got! You know mama's crackhead ass ain't going to do no shit for us! When you get the other part of that bread, put like a stack on my books so I'll have something to take with me when they move me up north, okay?"

The youngster then handed the phone back to Six.

Six told his girlfriend to do it right now, and that he would call her back in ten minutes to see where she was at with it. Asad gave Byrd $25,000 for the hit. He kept $8,000 and gave the rest to Six's girl for him to get it done. Now Six was paying his young hit man $10,000 of the $17,000 that was left.

"How old is your sister?"

"She's nineteen. About to be twenty in a few months. Why, you trying to get at her?"

"No nothing like that! You're family once you get this done. And that makes her family, feel me? I just wanted to know, because you know my girl dances, and she can put her on her shit so you won't have to worry about her too much. I'll have her back. This ain't no pimp-hoe shit, homie! We just getting that cash."

"Man, that's up to her. But I know she's been thinking about doing that shit, and I guess if she's going to do it, she should fuck with y'all."

"Cool, I'll tell my girl to put a bug in her ear."

"I think it'll be best to get that fool at rec. If I can do it without getting no more time, that's what I wanna do. But if I can't, fuck it, I ain't never going home anyway."

With that said, the deal was a lock.

Chapter 22

Last call for alcohol was announced through the speakers at Zarkos Nite Club. It was Zay's favorite time to be in the club, because it was ladies' night. He was privately celebrating his new boss status one month after Jasso's retirement from the streets.

A skimpy-dressed woman danced on the small dance floor next to the bar where Zay was seated watching her watch him. She made her way over to him just as the song ended.

"Don't you want to buy me a drink?" she asked, giving him a seductive smile.

Zay took in the sexually stimulating danky scent of her Prada perfume and every bit of her voluptuous body she had on display. She was dressed in a very short low-cut dress with the front open, showing off her butterfly tattoo and matching belly ring. Zay was ready to take her down right there.

"Sure, why not! I think you earned it. Tell him what you want. I got you, ma."

"Okay. Hey, bartender, can I get a Passion?"

"I have the Whipped Cream Smirnoff, but I'm out of the strawberries. I can use cherries? It's just as good."

"Okay! But if I don't like it, we not paying for it."

Zay laughed.

"If she don't like it, give us half price on one she would like. I know you got to get your money just like the rest of us."

"One house Passion coming up," the bartender said before going to make her drink.

"Ma, you can't do my boy like that. He really shouldn't still be making drinks for nobody. You must've missed them say last call when you were trying to seduce me with your dancing."

"Did it work? Because I was just getting warmed up."

"It's hard to say now that you said that. I think a boss needs to see what it do when you nice and hot," Zay flirted back while taking a sip of his Remy and coke. "What's your name? I feel it's one to remember."

"ShyAnn, but you can just call me Ann, because ain't nothing shy about me!"

"Here's you drink, hotness. I hope you enjoy it," the bartender told ShyAnn after handing her his version of the one she asked for.

He waited for her to take a sip before he moved on to finish cleaning up the bar area.

Zay paid and gave him a nice tip once she told

the bartender that she loved it. After introductions, they talked until they had to get out.

"You taking me home? I mean, you coming home with me? Because I ain't finished with you yet."

"Are you sure you want me to do that, because I wouldn't be coming over there just to talk," Zay explained, letting his intentions be known upfront while remotely starting his 1969 Buick Wildcat.

"Zay, you got me drunk and wet, so now you got to fix me. Will you at least talk dirty to me?" she asked, hanging on to him as they walked out to his car.

"This is me. Where you parked at?"

"I came with my friends, and they saw me with you, so they left me," she explained while climbing over the driver's seat to the passenger's side of his car.

He got in and pulled away from the club once she gave him her address. Zay was so lit, he did not care nor did he notice her texting on her phone. The only thing that was on his horny mind was getting between her long legs for the night. He parked in front of her address and then they walked arm in arm into the apartment building on Wells Street. Once the two of them were in the small elevator, they made out all the way up to her floor. Zay put passion marks on her neck.

"I can see you really like me!" ShyAnn giggled, rubbing the nice hard print in his jeans.

The elevator doors opened and she walked out ahead of him. Zay watched the sway of her hips, round butt, and fine long legs as he followed her.

She opened the door to the dimly lit apartment and led him inside and across the dining room. Zay got a funny feeling that something wasn't right, but he had his gun on him, so he wasn't worried too much.

"Ann, I'm going to fuck the understanding out of you. Give you just what you been begging for!"

He was all smiles as he thought of what she was going to look like naked.

"Hold on a sec! Let me go get a glass of water. You want one?" she asked, spinning out of his reach and heading toward the kitchen.

Suddenly, before Zay could answer, someone rushed him and knocked him to the floor. ShyAnn ran back out the way they came in. Her job was done. After the fight at Byrd's party, Summer had pointed out Zay to Eshy before she was rushed to the hospital. When she got home, Eshy asked her if she had a friend who was down to set up Zay for him. That's how Eshy met ShyAnn.

He paid her $2,000 to get Zay to the apartment. It took her a little over a month to get him to the death trap. ShyAnn did what she was paid to do and got out of there fast. She did not want to be anywhere around to witness whatever they had planned for Zay.

Being the shooter he was known to be, Zay was pulling his trigger before his back had even touched the floor. He killed the first would-be assassin and badly wounded another. He then saw a shadow move not far from the first man. Who it was didn't matter to Zay. It was kill or be killed, and his only concern was himself. When he got to his feet, Zay noticed that all his drinking had his balance off, but not so much that he couldn't defend himself.

The only light in the apartment came from the bare front window, so all Zay could make out were shadows of the remaining assailants. But Eshy could see him just fine. Eshy chambered his Mossberg bump to let Zay know what was coming at him next. When Zay turned toward the sound without pulling his own trigger, Eshy's big blast sent Zay slamming into the wall of the kitchen counter. Eshy walked up on Zay. He was followed by Von, who was the man who Zay had wounded when he sent blind shots into the darkness. They stood over him, and it was clear to them that Zay was dying from the sizable wound in his mid-section. But that wasn't good enough for them.

"Bitch! That was for the folks you just shot!" Eshy told him as he chambered another round. "And this one's for my nigga Freebandz, you pussy!"

Zay tried to speak, but only blood spilled from his lips. He tried to lift his gun, but his arms would not respond. Zay was helpless but unafraid as the next blast from the pump smeared away his face. Von emptied four shots into the lifeless body because of the pain he was feeling from getting grazed by Zay's shot.

"E, let's get the fuck out of here before them people get here."

Von looked down at Zay's mangled body and smiled.

"It's closed casket for his funeral, and we can dump that muthafucka down too, if you want to, fam. But we got to go now!"

Eshy agreed, and they eased down the back stairs to the floor below. They then took the front stairs out of the building, where they split up. They had already decided to meet back up at their getaway car that was parked on the next block.

142

Chapter 23

On day two of Ron being in the Milwaukee County jail, he fell in and out of sleep all night while anxiously anticipating his release. Whenever the third shift officer made a round through the cell block, Ron was up out of bed standing in his cell door window looking at the clock on the wall over the officer's station. He prayed they were there to pick him up and let him go.

In the morning when the doors opened, all the men lined up outside of their cell doors as usual until the officer finished giving the jail rules.

"No fighting. If you fight, you will be sent to the 4D, the box, or whatever you like to call it. If you fight, you will end up there, and you will be charged. So don't fight. If you want to be treated like grown men, then act like it! If you disrespect me, I'm going to get right with you. So let's try to keep it down in the dayroom. No flooding and no standing in anyone else's cell doorway. If I see you, you will be locked in for up to twenty-three hours. Don't cross this red line without my permission. If you do, I will shoot you. So please test me and step one of your bad asses over it."

The entire cellblock broke out in laughter at the homely, black female officer's comment about shooting them.

"I said keep it down. The day room's now open."

Officer Diggs was outnumbered and armed with only a small taser and a two-way radio. But she knew if she did not bother the inmates, they would not bother her. She was told on her first day on the job that no one likes an asshole. So she did her best not to be one unless she had to be. Diggs knew that the men and women in the jail had enough to stress about without the guards watching over them going out of their way to make it harder for them.

Ron decided not to get on the phone until after lunch, so he went into the gym that consisted of four basketball rims without nets and a few mats for those who wanted to do calisthenics. This morning, there were eight men running up and down the court barefooted playing a game of basketball. They had to play like this because the jail did not allow any kind of footwear except county-issued shower shoes, and it was very hard to play a game in them.

"Hey, I got next!" Ron called out to the men on the court.

He then went and found a spot against the wall to watch.

"Say, man, look out!" Lil' Larry called out when

Ron stepped over his legs to get by him instead of going around.

"What? Watch yourself, fam!"

Ron tried to bully the seventeen-year-old, sizing him up and thinking he could easily take the kid in a fight if it came down to it.

Lil' Larry sprung to his feet.

"You right, bitch-ass nigger!" he barked in response.

Ron never saw the shank coming. All he felt was the pain from Larry's multiple lightning-quick jabs. The first was to Ron's left side of his face; the next was to his neck. When Ron grabbed his neck wound and attempted to stop blood from spilling out too fast, Larry pounded the cruel weapon repeatedly into his body, before he calmly walked out of the now-empty gym and straight into the shower.

Dizzy from all his blood loss, Ron was still able to pick himself up off the floor and make it halfway to the gym exit before falling down for the last time. Officer Diggs found him dead when she did one of her routine safety rounds.

"Lock in! Everybody lock the fuck in now!" she ordered the men while hitting the panic button on her radio. "You heartless muthafuckas wrong! Y'all wrong!"

She was slightly in shock from finding Ron lying in a pool of blood. She never thought she would ever have to deal with something like this, but she did not have sympathy for snitches; and she had found out that Ron was waiting to be released to put in work for the detectives not long before she found him. So the death did not bother her as much as she was putting on for her bosses.

"Thanks for the paid time off!" she said to the corpse as the area filled with her fellow officers responding to the panic call.

~ ~ ~

Asad floated down Silver Spring doing over 50 mph after coming back from the meeting at the small airport. He wove Sky's rainbow-painted Lexus CT hybrid skillfully in and out of traffic. One of the city's finest did not see Asad's driving as tactful, but instead reckless, so he decided to pull over the SUV. Asad saw the car speed up behind him, so he slowed as he smashed out the wine Black & Mild he had been smoking. He also turned down Chris Brown's latest hits. He did not want to give the police any other reason to hold him up.

Just as Asad had expected, the cop car's emergency lights lit up, so he pulled over and stopped the SUV just the way he was supposed to do in such a situation. He was glad he still did not have the $1.5 million in the car, just in case they got on one with him and made him get out so they could search the Lexus.

An attractive, short-haired, white female cop walked up and knocked on the driver's door and then on the window for him to let it down.

"Whose car is this?" she asked, showing her disappointment in finding a man in the driver's seat.

Asad noticed she proudly wore her rainbow charm around her neck. What he didn't know was that she was hoping to find the woman she met at Pride Fest in Chicago a few weeks before.

"It belongs to a friend of mine. Is there something wrong with it?" Asad asked, handing her his information.

"What's this friend's name?" She was already running the plates. "It's Skylar Baker."

"So, it's Skylar!" she repeated with a smile, before she walked back to her car to run a background check on Asad.

About twenty minutes went by before Asad started wondering why there was such a holdup. Suddenly, two black Chevy TrailBlazers pulled up in front and on the side of him to block any chance of Asad pulling off. Officers poured out from the SUVs with their guns ready.

"Asad King! Put your hands out the window and open the door from the outside."

He did as he was told.

"Get on the ground now!" they ordered from all directions at once.

Asad was shocked and confused, but he did as he was told. He was then kicked in his ribs and roughly put in cuffs by a bear of a cop. After that, he was helped to his feet and placed in the back of one of the black SUVs.

"Can somebody tell me what the hell is going on?" he asked as they pulled away from the scene and headed toward downtown.

"You have the right to remain silent, so use it!" the officer informed him.

Asad knew this was about more than the little speeding he was doing. Now knowing he was not going to get any answers from either of his escorts, he decided to take the officer's advice, but he still wondered what was going on.

Once they made it to the station, Asad was placed in a windowless room by himself with only a table that was bolted to the concrete floor and three chairs. He sat in one of the chairs and prepared for whatever they came at him with next. After an hour, two detectives entered the room, both of them tall and tired looking. The first man was black with slightly graying hair and was named Price. The other white detective had low-cut, dirty brown hair and very pale skin and was named Saveson.

"Here comes the good cop, bad cop bullshit!"

Asad mumbled to himself.

"Do you need anything to drink, eat, or smoke?" Saveson asked, taking a seat on the edge of the table.

"Yeah, water," Asad told him while sitting back in the chair.

Detective Price opened the door and gave Asad's order to someone in the hall, and within seconds, someone else walked in with a glass of water.

"Sorry, we're out of bottles," Price replied as he handed Asad a paper cup.

Asad did not reply to the detective; he just drank the water and stared from one to the other as they questioned him over and over about how he made his money. But the only response they received from Asad was him asking for his attorney. With that, the detectives walked out of the room and left him alone again. It was hours later until Asad saw another face, and that was an officer who came and took him to be Mirandized, photographed, fingerprinted, and booked into the jail. To his surprise, he did not have to sit in the stinky and overcrowded booking room for very long.

Asad was taken straight to a cell block on the sixth floor. He passed a clock that read 12:35 a.m. before he was placed in a single cell. Knowing he could not find out anything more than he was told already, he made the bed and called it a night.

"I knew I was due for a vacation, but not like this.

I'm going to have to talk to somebody about the food in the place," Asad joked to himself as he picked through the cold bag of food the officer gave him on the way to the cell.

Chapter 24

Sky had been spending a lot of time at Asad and China's place lately. Everything between them was going great, mostly because they did not think about it and just went with the flow of their new relationship. This was not how Sky had thought of being with Asad, but she loved having her cake with steak.

The surprised ringing of her home phone gave her the timeout she needed from trying to decide what outfits to pack for her stay at the apartment.

"Hello, this is Detective Mavric. I'm calling to speak to a Ms. Skylar Baker."

Sky looked at the number on the caller ID as she muted the radio.

"Yes, this is her," she answered, thinking he was going to tell her they caught the guy who had killed Penny.

"Ms. Baker, do you own a multiple-colored Lexus CT?"

"Yes, why?"

Her heart raced with anticipation of bad news.

"Did you allow anyone to use your car, and can

you tell me his or her name?" the detective asked in a business-like manner.

Sky saw flashing lights and ran to the window to see if it was Asad pulled over by the detective that was calling her. She saw that it was not her Lexus, but one of the cars she always saw racing up and down her block.

"Yes, I let my—my—"

This was the first time she was asked about the relationship between her and Asad, and she did not know the proper way to answer it.

"My boyfriend has it. I let him use it today. His name is Asad King. Is he alright?"

"Okay! Well, King has been taken into custody, and this is a courtesy call to let you know that you can pick your car up at 41st and Silver Spring. But if you're not here within the next half hour to forty-five minutes, it will be towed at your expense. And, Ms. Baker, I don't think you want such a nice car sitting in the city tow lot," Mavric explained, trying his best to convince her to get there so he could try to pump her for information.

"I'm on my way now. But you didn't say why Asad is going to jail," she inquired while looking for her cell phone.

"You tell me, Ms. Baker. Why do you think your boyfriend is in jail?"

Sky could hear the smile in his voice.

"I'll be there shortly to pick up my car. Thank you!"

She ended the call, and then called China's job and left a message for her to call her back ASAP. She then called Zay a few times with no luck on him answering.

"Come on, Zay! Call me back. This ain't the time for this!" Sky said to herself before calling Tasha to come give her a ride to pick up her car.

"What up, Sis? I was just about to call you."

"Tasha, tell me you at home and can come take me to go get my car?"

"I was just walking out to go to the store, but I'm on my way to you now. What's wrong?"

"I don't know. Asad got pulled over or some shit. I don't know what for, but this crank-ass detective called me to come get my car before he has it towed. I think he just wants to see if he can get some info out of me about Asad," Sky explained while slipping her feet back into her shoes.

~ ~ ~

Detective Mavric had just finished searching the Lexus for the third time. He was eager to find anything to build a case against Asad, just in case his star witness had cold feet when the time came. Mavric was taking a chance pulling Asad in before the play was put into action, but he knew he had to get the man who would be his ticket into the FBI.

Sky spotted the plain-clothed officer as Tasha parked in front of the Lexus.

"Excuse me, are you the detective that I talked to on the phone?" Sky asked when she got out of the car.

"Yes! You must be Skylar Baker." The detective shook her hand. "Can we talk before you go? I won't take up too much of your time."

He gave Sky his best phony smile.

"Sure! Can you tell me where Asad is and why he was put in jail?" Sky asked, taking her keys out of Mavric's big hand.

He walked Sky back to his cruiser and offered her a seat inside. When she refused, he knew picking her for information was not going to be as easy as he had hoped it would be.

"What does Asad do for a living?"

Sky's phone started vibrating in her hand. When she looked at the screen, she saw it was a text from Jasso. She told him to meet her at her house, because she could not explain now.

"Detective, why does any of that matter if he was pulled over for speeding? I mean, I can see if he was driving without a license, but I've never known anyone to go to jail for driving a few miles over the limit."

"Like I said, he fits the description of a person of interest."

"Interest to what?"

"I can't tell you that; but if you cooperate with me, I can get this all cleared up."

"Well, detective, the only thing I can tell you is that I'm sure Asad isn't the person of interest you're looking for. Thank you for calling me about my car, and could you tell Asad that I'll be there to get him as soon as I can?"

Sky then turned and began walking back to her car.

"Ms. Baker?"

Sky stopped and turned back around to face the detective.

"Do you mind if I have a look in your car before you go?"

"Come on now, detective. We both know you guys have been all through it way before I got here; and before you lie, let me tell you that I saw you closing the door before we pulled up."

"Have a good day, Ms. Baker."

Sky stepped into her car and quickly pulled away, with her sister right behind her. Mavric took down Tasha's plate number so he could run it later. When Sky turned down her block, Jasso and Amanda were there waiting for her. Sky told her sister she would call her later so she could leave, and then she took her friends into the house. Once they were seated inside, she told them about the detective and explained that she felt he was fishing for something that he was not telling her.

"Don't trip! I already put the lawyer on it when I got your text telling me he was in jail. He should find out everything real soon. I also called Roberto to see if they took care of things on their end. He said they did, so this is some whole other shit!" Jasso explained. "This might have something to do with ol' boy who got knocked."

"Who, Ronnie?" Sky asked.

"Yeah! I wouldn't put it past him. But hopefully we don't got to worry about him talking if all went as planned."

"Hey, have you talked to Zay? I've been calling and texting his ass since before I went to get my car."

"I was just about to ask you the same thing. I'll have the lawyer check in and see if he got locked up too," Jasso told her.

Jasso and Amanda then walked out the front door, leaving Sky wondering what was really going on.

Chapter 25

Two teens stumbling upon a sight straight out of a horror film was what sparked the homicide investigation that was now going on inside the apartment building on Wells Street.

"I know that must've been hard for you to see, and I wish I could do something to make the memory of it go away. But I can't," the homicide detective said to the young girl who discovered the bodies in the apartment. "It will be a great help to me if you will walk me through how you came across this mess. Every little detail could help put whoever did this behind bars."

The girl looked for permission from her mother before she said a word. The girl's mother gave her the okay to go ahead.

"Me and him were just roaming the halls."

"Excuse me, but who is him?" the detective asked as he made notes on the small pad in his hands.

"Oh, Keshun. The boy they're talking to over there."

"This might sound stupid, but how do you two know each other?"

"We just friends. He's in some of my classes at school."

"So you two were just looking for some place to fool around when you found the apartment?"

"No, we wasn't trying to fool around. We just friends," she corrected the prying and sneaky detective.

The detective let the girl finish telling her story before he then went to question the building manager, who told him that he was always running kids out of the vacant apartment. The manager told him he did notice the door was open when he was on his way to do some repairs on another floor. But before he could get back to it, the kids found him and told him about the bodies.

But what the slimy manager did not tell the detective was that a month ago Eshy had paid him in drugs and cash to use the place as a stash spot. Eshy made sure the greedy manager never saw the face behind the payment, just the ones who gave it to him. The manager did not care as long as his high was free and he made a little money out of the deal.

The case of the faceless body was not going to be an easy one to crack. Just as the detective was about to go back into the bloody apartment, an officer stopped him holding a wallet that was surely stripped of its cash and/or cards but still contained the driver's license of its owner. The detective was sure it belonged to the faceless victim.

~ ~ ~

The girls went to work trying to find out what they could about Asad after the lawyer told them he was being held on summary charges. There was nothing the attorney could do at the time but wait for the assistant district attorney to meet with him or let Asad go. China went online and found out the jail's visiting hours and dates. She then made reservations for them to visit Asad as soon as they could. Sky was on the phone making sure he was still being held in the county jail and had not been moved out to the house of corrections for unsafe keeping.

~ ~ ~

China and Sky arrived at the visitor center almost an hour before the check-in time, so they could beat the line. However, they found a few other women had the same plan. So Sky paid the three women $20 each for their places in line.

"Hi, we're here to see Asad King," China told the lazy-looking male officer sitting behind the check-in window.

The officer casually tapped on his keyboard and then asked, "Are you sure he's in our jail, ma'am, because I don't see him in our logs."

"Yeah, we're sure he's here. Y'all gave me a visiting time, didn't you?" China answered him, clearly getting upset.

Sky took over the conversation before China got them kicked out or thrown in jail themselves.

"They told us we could come see him today. So are you sure you're spelling his name right?"

Sky then proceeded to spell it for the officer, and this time he turned the computer monitor around so they could watch him put in the name.

"He was brought in on Friday," China informed him while taking deep breaths to calm herself.

"Okay, you're right! I'm sorry! I must have been spelling it wrong. He is here, but you can't see him at this time because the floor he's on is on lockdown pending investigation of the inmate death that I'm sure you've heard about by now."

Ron's murder was all over the news and front pages of the papers, because things like that did not happen often in the jail. The girls had not paid mind to it because of their concern for their man.

~ ~ ~

After the two women arrived back home, they took care of some busy work to keep their minds from stressing over Asad as much as they could. But then Sky received a call from Jasso telling her that Zay was found dead in an apartment somewhere on Wells. This news made the bad day even worse.

"We should give his family a call and let them know we're here for them if they need anything," China suggested to Sky.

"I'm sure Jasso let them know that and is going to take care of everything. We should just give them some time and pay our respects at his funeral. I don't need nobody blaming me for nothing right now!" Sky explained while letting tears fall for her friend.

Chapter 26

The following evening, Sky received a call from Luis asking her who was going to be at the truck stop to pick up the monthly package now that Zay was gone.

"My dear, I'm sorry. But he is already on his way there. This was all last minute for me as well, so when Jasso called me, my guy was already gone," Luis explained.

"Okay, don't worry! I can handle it," Sky assured him, not wanting to mess up their arrangement. After ending the call, Sky turned to China and said, "China, that was the boss man himself on the phone." This was the first time that Luis had ever called her directly.

"Oh shit! What now?" China asked in the middle of folding the wash.

"He wanted to know who was going to meet the guy with the work, and the best part is, he's already on his way."

"Well, if he's on his way, bitch, we just going to have to go get it our damn selves. Do you know where we got to go?"

"I'm glad you're feeling that way, because that's

kind of what I told him just now," Sky admitted before taking a nice pull off her blunt. "I'm texting him now for the address and telling him I'll be there to meet him personally."

Sky knew Luis really did not care who made the meeting, just as long as it was not the Feds and he got his money in the end. Jasso made sure Luis knew all that was going on, because if things went bad, it all fell back on him. The girls knew this as well and did not want any trouble from Luis or Jasso.

~ ~ ~

Sky drove down to the Illinois state line just in time in the dark gray Pontiac G6 they had rented for the trip. China thought the trip seemed like a grade-school field trip. They were both charged with excitement, since this was the first time either of them had made this meeting.

"I guess you two sweet little ladies are here for me?"

The girls looked toward the voice and found a short, dingy-looking Mexican man showing off his tobacco-stained smile.

"No, I don't think so. Keep it moving!" China told him.

"No, I don't think you want me to do that without giving me this car. I—I!"

163

"What! Muthafucka! I said get the fuck away from here before I blow your funky balls off!" China snapped as she pulled her gun on him.

That's when Sky remembered that they were supposed to give the rental to the guy they were meeting at the truck stop.

"Hold up, boo! I think this is our man," she told China, pushing her hand down for her to lower the gun.

"Hey, buddy, are you Miguel?"

"I was when I woke up this morning."

His smile returned.

"I told you that you were waiting on me. What did you girls think—that I would be holding a sign or something?" Miguel laughed at his own joke.

"No, we're sorry. There's just been so many guys trying to talk to us since we've been here waiting on you," Sky apologized while getting out of the car.

"I saw that!"

"How long have you been here watching us?" China asked once she also stepped out of the car.

"Long enough to know that you wasn't followed. Now, let's get this over with. I got a long drive home," he informed the two.

He also told them that the next time they'd meet they should look for him inside the diner.

~ ~ ~

Driving on the way back home was a different story for the girls. They were now in a big Chevy dually that they traded with Miguel for the rental. China made him promise not to tell Luis about her pulling a gun on him. Miguel also said that he would call them and walk them through getting the product out of the hidden compartment of the truck as soon as Luis let him know they made it home safely.

"How in the hell did Zay do this by himself?" China asked, fighting herself to keep her eyes open.

"Girl, you know bro-bro be gone off the rollers and shit. His ass used to be up for days at a time!" Sky replied.

"It's fucked up what happened to him. I miss his crazy butt. He was cool as hell!"

"Yeah, but Zay was a straight-up killa, for real. We used to smoke together when he insisted on riding with me to serve someone new or to pick up money from somebody that owed me. Yeah, anyway, Zay used to tell me stories about what he did to muthafuckas, which made me glad he was on our side!"

Sky then yawned, causing China to do the same.

"Do you think all that's been happening to us is connected somehow? I'm just saying! It's all been back-to-back, and I can't help but look for a connection that I know ain't there," China said, explaining what was on her mind while trying to keep Sky awake.

She even let the window down, hoping the cool early-morning air would help.

They tried everything they could think of to fight off the drowsiness. Sky had dozed off, but was shocked awake when China veered over the side of the road's rigged markers.

"Girl, you up?" she asked nervously.

"I'm good! I'm good!"

China shook her head and then slammed down a five-hour energy drink for the boost that she needed.

Sky settled down and cranked up the radio in hopes that the loud music would help them stay awake. But when China's head bobbed for the third time in less than ten minutes, she made her pull over and she took the wheel, only to find out that she was not in much better condition to drive.

They made it to the oasis and parked in the rest area to do just that before they killed themselves. They both got out and stretched their legs and used the restroom. Then they bought more snacks and fresh drinks.

Once they were back inside the truck, Sky closed her eyes and was down for the count. The energy drinks had kicked in for China, so she was ready to go. Besides, she did not trust the thirsty-looking truckers enough to close her eyes, so she locked the doors, eased back on the road, and got them home in one piece.

"Sky! Sky!" China tried to wake her up, but she didn't move. "Bitch! Wake the hell up with your good-snoring ass!" she yelled, hitting Sky playfully in the arm.

"I'm up! I was just resting my eyes."

"Resting your eyes, my ass! Bitch, you was asleep! We at home already, so call our boy and let him know that we good!" China told her as she pulled into an empty parking slot at her building.

Sky looked around. She was amazed that she had slept long enough for them to be at the apartment already.

"Why you bring us here?"

"It's the only place to park this big-ass truck without it getting towed or fucked with, until we do what we have to do with it."

"Good thinking!"

Sky then made the call and told Luis she would call in the morning to get the instructions needed to open the stash spots of the truck.

Chapter 27

The lockdown had been lifted at the county jail. Listening to the guys talking on the cell block all night told Asad that the lockdown was because the officer in the pod across from them had found Ron dead in the gym. All he did was smile to himself, knowing that he did not have that part to worry about anymore.

"Mr. King, I need to see your wristband," the pretty female officer said, which woke him up.

"What?" he asked while sitting up in his bunk.

"Could you show me your wristband, please? You have to come to me. I cannot come to you."

He walked over and did as she asked. He then remained standing in his doorway looking around to see who he knew on the block.

"Hey, do you know when we can order phone cards?" he asked the guy in the cell next to him.

"We should get them today, but if you put a slip in today, you will get it tomorrow."

Asad thanked him by giving him his breakfast tray, before going back to bed until it was time to place his order for canteen. He wondered when the detectives were going to come and try to talk to him again. It was clear to Asad that Detective Mavric was not going to give up just because he gave him the silent treatment. He knew he would have to think of a way to make Mavric stop coming after him.

~ ~ ~

Amanda's best friend, Saleena, owned a small cleaning service. She held a contract to clean offices for the county courthouse. Last night one of Saleena's employees called in sick, thus leaving her to step in for her at the last minute. In order for her to maintain the Ms. Independent diva status that Saleena loved so much, she sometimes had to put in work herself. She started the business by herself before she met and hired Amanda at one of their children's school functions. Jasso made Amanda quit when she almost miscarried their second child. After that incident, Amanda helped Saleena team up with the Welfare Work Search Program and was blessed to find eight hard-working young mothers who were still working for her now, four years later.

The third floor banked the offices of the district attorneys. Saleena ran through the ten offices like the professional she was, until she was finishing up the last room and came across Jasso's name on some paperwork in the trash. When she picked it up, she saw that it had Asad's name on it as well. What she found were the transcripts of Ron's first and last talks of making a deal for his freedom. Saleena passed the papers on to her best friend's husband along with a bill from the district attorney's car insurance company that gave Jasso not just the attorney's home address but also the names of his wife and children. For the information, Jasso gave Saleena $5,000 and a new work van. Asad knew that this was a very small price to pay for his freedom.

~ ~ ~

ADA Sam Brown sat in his big corner office with the two-overworked drug task force detectives. He was listening to them try to convince him not to drop their case and release Asad. What they didn't know was that there was nothing they could tell ADA Brown to get him to keep the case open. Brown had received a box of long-stem black roses at his home with photos of him having dinner with his wife, and others showing his kids walking to school. The one that made him play along was the one of his daughter's badly beaten boyfriend with a note that read: "Drop everything that has anything to do with the King case, or the next person we touch will be all of the ones you love."

"Just keep King in a few days longer. I'm sure

there's someone who will take the get-out-of-jail-free card to give up the person who killed our witness," Moore stated.

"And once we have him, I know he will give up King and his buddies to save his ass," Mavric jumped in, trying to help his partner sell their plan to Brown.

"Look, it's not going to happen! So unless either of you have anything new. I mean new hard evidence —" Brown paused to give the detectives a chance to speak up. Not that it would have changed his mind, but for show. "—release King ASAP, and I don't want to see either of you in front of me about him again!" he ordered after seeing the dumb looks on their faces.

After a week in the county jail Asad was released in the middle of the night, and to his surprise, Jasso was outside the jail to pick him up along with Amanda, China, and Sky.

Chapter 28

Milwaukee's number one new favorite local rap star, Resco, threw himself a going-away party at Club Brooklyn. He opened the mic up for other local artists to get their shine on in front of a packed club.

~ ~ ~

Because you only live once is what my homie told me
And there a life after death is what the preacher showed me
So I'm in and out of trouble like my conscious-ness is doubled-visioned
And I just can't separate this way of living
I stash away some cash for the weekend
So I can blow some bud and pop bottles with my current friends
All I ever thought about was dollar signs and sleepin' in
And now I'm lookin' at my life from a Wisconsin pen . . . Damn!
I should of known that even life got a reflex

*I was fooled, the streets played it cool and hit me
with a pretext*
    *Was caught up in a wave of deceit but never the
loss*
    *Continued running wicked in the street, so guess
what happen next*
    I'm livin' so reckless . . .

~ ~ ~

Asad allowed the girls to take him out to this event after he was released from the county jail.

"What up, fam? I should've known something like this would bring money out!" Cash said as he greeted everyone when he approached Asad's table.

"No, man! That's you, Mr. Cash Up Front. I'm a lil' nigga out with the girls. They wanted to see the show. You know me. If it ain't about money, I ain't about it!" Asad responded as they shook hands.

Cash said hello to Sky and China before resuming his conversation with Asad.

"Yeah, I'm here with my niggas. That's their family MJ on stage now. He's going to be the next to blow."

~ ~ ~

I'm reckless . . . Reckless.

I load the cannon in front of my kid
She looking at me like Daddy why you living so
reckless
Because I'm out there, baby, trying to feed my
family
And these streets wanna jam me 'cause I'm
reckless
So why are we trying so hard to live when I'm
only gonna live reckless? . . .

~ ~ ~

"I got a mixtape with him on it. I was hoping he did this song. I forgot the name, but this shit hot!" Asad told him while refilling his glass with champagne from one of the three bottles sitting on his table.

Asad then excused himself from the girls and walked away to talk with Cash.

~ ~ ~

At least you've learned your lesson, count your
blessings
Instead of having tunnel vision, see the bigger
picture
And always know that just over the rainbow
There's something waiting for you, I can show

174

you and you know it
But I'm still livin' reckless, so be patient with me.

~ ~ ~

"Hey, fam, MJ going to have to do another song because they ain't ready yet," Eshy told Cash when he walked up on him talking with Asad.

The sight of Eshy made Asad's head hurt. It felt like something was trying to bust out. Asad remembered a slim red-bone female with long hair with Eshy, who introduced herself to him as Summer.

Asad then remembered being stomped in the face. All this flashed through Asad's mind.

"Man, do I know you from somewhere?" he asked Eshy.

"Shit, fam! I be all over the place and everywhere fucking with music shit. So we may've crossed paths a time or two," Eshy lied, and then told Cash he would meet him at the table.

He did not want to be around Asad any longer than he had to be. Eshy had robbed so many people, places, and things over the past few years that he could not remember all their faces, and there was no way he was taking a chance with his life.

"Cash, man, I'll give you a call tomorrow sometime. I got to get back to the table before they come looking for a nigga. You know how women get about their QT."

"Alright, make sure you do that. I should be ready for you by then anyway."

"I got you. Just let me know then."

They shook hands again, and Asad made his way back to his table, all the while looking over the crowd as he went. He wanted to catch another glimpse of Eshy.

"What's wrong with you Asad?" Sky asked while getting China's attention.

"I got a little headache. I'm good though."

"No, bae. You look pale. Do you want to go home?" China asked as she wiped sweat from his face.

"No, no. I'm good y'all. I just need some of this water."

He took a drink from one of their bottled waters on the table.

The music and comedy show were well worth the money. Asad and the girls laughed until they cried; but on the way home Asad thought back on the night when he got jumped.

"Muthafucka!"

The girls stopped talking and turned to see what Asad was cussing about.

"What you see?" Sky asked, looking out her window and getting ready to toss the blunt she was holding.

"One of them bitch-ass niggas that jumped me was at the club with Cash tonight."

"So what you going to do, bae?"

"I don't know yet. But as soon as I saw him, my head started pounding and I kind of remembered shit!" Asad explained as he continued to drive home.

"Fuck all that! We can deal with that shit another time. The big issue is you remembered something from then!" Sky said with excitement.

"Yeah, I did, didn't I?" Asad smiled. "Are we staying at your house tonight?"

"I don't know. China, are you spending the night with us or what?" Sky asked, licking her lips and smiling at her.

China had been staying at Sky's place since Asad went to jail. The only time she went home was when Sky's hustle wouldn't let her get away. To China, it was just the same as being home with Asad when he would have to stay out until the early morning hours.

"Bitch, don't play! You know what's going on. But y'all can feed me first before we do anything else."

"That sounds like a George Webb Restaurant call to me."

"Bae, you know it is!" China answered Asad as she took the blunt from Sky and took in a deep pull of the weed.

Once they arrived at the restaurant Asad dropped the girls off so they could get a booth and place their orders while he parked the car. After they finished eating, they all went back to Sky's place for the night, where the three of them made love together for the first time since Asad's release.

Afterward Asad was unable to sleep from all the thoughts that were rushing through his mind. He slid from between his two sleeping beauties and then took a shower, hoping it would clear his mind.

When that didn't work, he dressed and made his way to the storage unit as if something was pulling him to his car. Once he sat inside his Grandville, he rolled a blunt before he rolled out to put the car back in storage. It was like being on autopilot. He went inside his unit and right to the money that he had stashed away—the same money that he could not remember since he had been released from the hospital.

"How in the fuck could I forget this?" he asked himself after doing a quick count and then putting it back where he found it.

He parked the car back in its storage unit, but then he realized he didn't have a way back home, so he grabbed his phone.

"What's up, creep?" Sky asked Asad, with the sound of a car door being closed in the background.

"I need you to come get me. Where you at?"

"Home. Just getting in the car. China got called in to work, so I'm about to take her to the apartment so she can get ready to go. Her ass didn't want to go, but I told her to go because we're going to be busy today. Now where'd you run off to that you need a ride?"

She already knew, because China had tracked his phone. But Sky didn't want to be the one that told him that.

"I'm at my storage unit. I came to put the car up and forgot y'all brought me up here to get it."

Sky laughed. "I'm on my way as soon as I drop China off."

They got off the phone, and when Sky and China both got in the car, Sky explained to China where Asad had gone.

"Just when we thought he was making some progress!" China joked.

"I didn't tell him that we knew where he was. You better tell him about his phone. I don't want him mad at me because of it."

"I will, but he won't be mad. He knows how I get," China explained as Sky headed downtown.

Chapter 29

Cash pulled his Camaro to a stop in front of the home he now shared with Summer and her kids. He stretched his tired body and then slid out of the car. Every muscle in his back ached from the long, nonstop drive he had just made from northern Wisconsin. He went up there to drop off two girls he had booked in the clubs for the next week.

It was now after 4:00 a.m. and Cash was dead tired, but not so much so that he didn't notice the full-sized Chevy Explorer van that was parked with its motor running two cars behind him.

Cash could tell there was someone inside, but the windows were too dark to see who it was. He pulled out his gun as he walked into the house, before going to investigate the van, after noticing the light on in his home. He wondered if Summer knew who was in the suspicious-looking van. He hurried up the porch steps, unlocked the door with the keyless entry remote system, and stepped inside.

"What up, fam?" Eshy greeted Cash, turning away from Summer, who was standing in front of him in her bed clothes.

"What's good, Eshy? Why in the fuck are you here at this time of the morning?" Cash asked as he quickly searched Summer's expression for any sign of guilt. "Them fools out there in that van must be with you?" he asked suspiciously.

Summer noticed the gun in his hand and backed away from Eshy a bit more, after realizing how it might look to him. Eshy noticed it as well.

"Yeah, that's me out there. What you got the banger out for, my nig? It's all love this way, fam."

"Shit! I didn't know who the fuck was outside my shit this late. Better safe than dead, feel me?" Cash replied, putting the gun away. "But what's good? You still ain't told me why you're here," he said after closing the door.

"I just had to come tell sis that I handled that fuck boy Zay for my nigga. RIP. So her and the kids can know the nigga ain't living good walking the streets while Freebandz is six feet deep in the ground."

"When did all this happen? I was just with you earlier."

"Shit! About a week or so ago. I caught that bitch-ass nigga drunk and slipping up after coming from a club. I handled that shit myself," Eshy explained, leaving out the full details of what had happened the night he ambushed Zay in the apartment building.

"I'm here this early because I'm about to jump

on the highway to take my brother-in-law to the Chi so he can see his PO. Then we gonna head down to ATL to do a little sightseeing. I'm thinking about moving down there with the wife and kids. I heard there's a real good cancer hospital there, and now that I got my shit under control, I want to get somewhere so I can beat this shit."

"I feel you, fam!" Cash agreed, shaking his head at the thought of his friend fighting cancer. "Well you be easy on that E-way. Them hoes out there bad. I saw plenty of muthafuckas pulled over on my way home just now," Cash warned him as he walked him out the door.

"I'm going back to bed, bae. Shy, thanks for doing what you did. You're a good friend, and be careful," Summer said on her way to their bedroom before he could respond.

"When you get this big-ass van?" Cash asked.

"About three weeks ago. I'm just now bringing it out because I had to have the sounds and TVs put in," Eshy explained.

"This bitch is nice! What's them, 26's?"

"You know it! They went right on, and this hoe rides like a brand new 'Lac, my nig."

"Make sure you hit me when you make it back so I can check it out. I might want to get me one and shit."

They said a few more words before Eshy promised to get with him as soon as he got back in town. Then he went and climbed in the van and drove off into the morning light.

No longer feeling as tired as he did when he first pulled up, Cash walked up to the bedroom and was turned on by Summer's very sexy sheer see-through teddy.

"What? Why you looking at me like that?" she asked when he walked into the room.

Cash didn't respond. He just climbed on the bed and pushed her legs apart, and then buried his face between them. Her eyes rolled from his skillful tongue. Summer moaned his name loud enough for the neighbors to know it. Wanting to share what she was feeling, Summer slid away from Cash's tongue work. She hurriedly undressed him, straddled his chest, and then took all of him in her warm mouth as he went back to work on making her cum. They 69'd their way deep into their bedroom festivities.

"Cash, do you really believe Eshy got the person that killed Free?" Summer asked, while lying on her lover's chest after they were spent from their morning sex.

"I knew you were thinking about that."

Cash pushed her hair out of his face.

"I can't say for sure, but I know if Eshy says he did, then there's a good chance it was done and he had a hand in it."

"Should I tell the kids?"

"I don't think that's a good thing to do. Just let them be as they are for now, and if one of them asks you one day about him, then you'll have a story with a happy ending for them," Cash told her before getting out of the bed to go to the bathroom.

Chapter 30

Asad was met at the door by his mother's little schnauzer, Bobby, whose bark was bigger than he was.

"Hey, Bobby, is you happy to see me? Have you been watching the house?" Asad asked the dog as he rubbed his soft fur.

"Ma, where you at?" he yelled from the door.

"Asad, is that you? I'm in the kitchen," Ms. King answered. "Boy, you know you need to get over here to see me more than you do. You act like you don't got no mama."

"Ma, stop it! I call you almost every day," he told her while walking toward the table for some Louisiana crunch cake.

"That's not the same. I be wanting to see your face. But it's okay, I got me a man now!" she let out with a little giggle.

"What? Stop playing with me. When you get this man, and where is he, so I can check him out."

"I've been talking to Fred for a few months now. We met down at bingo," she began as she poured Asad a glass of milk to go with his cake. "He might be your step-daddy," she joked as she sat down with him at the table.

"What! I got to meet this nigga before any of that happens. Is he here now?" he asked, not finding anything funny in what she was telling him.

It wasn't that Asad didn't want his mother to date; he just didn't want her to be taken advantage of or hurt.

"Ha, ha! You going to have a white daddy!" Ms. King teased her son while really starting to laugh now.

The phone rang before she could tease him anymore.

"Hello. This is her. Oh God! No! How?" she questioned the caller.

Asad noticed the change in her voice and the expression on her face.

"What is it? Who is that on the phone?" he asked as he reached over for it.

She hung up before he could get the phone from her.

"Asad. That was . . . it was . . . your father died last night," she finally got the words out.

"What are you talking about?"

"Your daddy was rushed to St. Michael's Hospital last night, but he died before he got there," she explained before she broke down crying.

Asad held his mother as she mourned for the man

who left her to fend for herself with a young Asad to care for. Ms. King raised him alone and struggled to give him the best life she could on her own. Asad wondered how she could be so distraught over him. But what he did not know was that his mother had chosen to be the other woman to his father's wife. Ms. King stopped playing along when she found out she was pregnant with Asad's big brother. After he was born, she was lonely and craved for her baby daddy to be in her son's life. This soon brought them together again, and they rekindled their sex life until their first-born son was killed in the accident.

Asad wondered why he felt a stabbing pain in his chest for the man who he did not really know. They saw each other over the years, but Asad was not up for his father being in and out of his life, so he simply stopped trying. But that didn't stop his heart from breaking just a little for him.

~ ~ ~

The funeral service held for Earl Williams took place in a small church on the corner of 29th and Galeana. It was the same church in which his mother's funeral was held. Mr. Williams's polished, dark-wood coffin was set in the center of the church in front of the main altar, for all to see and pay their last respects. Ms. King, Asad, China, and Fred sat in the far back row of the church. Sky could not make it because she was home sick, and she did not do very well at funerals.

When the preacher sang his last song, he called everyone up to say a few words about the deceased. That was when a darker version of Asad took the microphone followed by two grief-stricken little girls. Asad soon found out that the three were his step-brother and step-sisters.

"Asad, go up there and stand for your father with them," Ms. King ordered her son, standing up so he could get past her from his seat.

He did as he was told, knowing this was not the time or place to protest. At his father's casket, the two brothers silently stared at each other for a few moments. This was the first time they had been face to face in years. The last time was when Mr. Williams tried to take Asad to a Bucks game. But Asad had declined to go when he saw that it was not going to be just him and his father.

"Hello, everybody, I'm Asad King, for all of you who don't know. I came to pay my last respects to my father and to stand for the King family. I don't have much to say, because I didn't allow myself to enjoy my dad's time on this earth when I was growing up. Now I want him to know I love him and wish I could take it all back and spend every moment with him."

Asad then turned to his step-brother.

"Bro, it's up to us to be the men our father wanted us to be. We have to be strong for our mothers and sisters."

With that said, the four of them hugged each other, which made a sad day a little more tolerable.

A wave of cars and trucks, along with the Cobra Motorcycle club to which their dad belonged followed the limousines as they slowly moved through the streets to the cemetery. Mr. Williams was placed in the ground next to his mother.

~ ~ ~

Asad's mother didn't attend the repass held in the beautifully decorated hall on the corner of 42nd and Capital Drive. Queena and Tahyra took to Asad right away. They would not let him get far away from them. He found out that his sister Queena was fourteen, just a year older than Tahyra. Both of them were true beauties and would be a handful. The girls wore their hair wrapped with light brown highlights that brought out their eyes. Their caramel complexions were flawless, and they had the singing voices of angels. Asad found this out when they sang for their father as his casket was being lowered into the ground.

"Bro, how do you deal with these two?" Asad

asked, hiding playfully behind Fame, who was just a few years younger than him.

"I don't know. All they do is hit me up for cash. That's all their little nappy-head butts want: money for this and that."

Asad ducked Tahyra's wild right hand as she attempted to slap Fame for saying her hair was nappy.

"Okay, so that's how I can get a break from y'all," Asad said while reaching into his pocket.

"No, it's going to be good, but we want to know everything about you. So there's no getting rid of us!" Queena spoke up.

Asad handed each of them $50.

"Okay, I can help you with that too. See that girl standing over there looking at the photos? Her name is China, and she's my girlfriend, so she can tell you all you want to know while I talk to your brother."

"Fame is your brother too," Tahyra reminded him after she took the money.

Then she and her sister went to question China, which allowed the brothers to talk with one another.

"I'm telling you now, if you keep that up them two are going to break you fast."

"It's okay. It's my time to spoil them. Since we're on the subject of money, I want to do my part in helping pay for things. I don't know how things are for y'all, but he was my dad too, so this falls on all of us."

"Asad, you don't have to do that. But I know I can't stop you, so you're going to have to talk to my mother about it. She won't tell me what she needs help with, so whatever you do, you're just going to have to put it in her hands," Fame explained to him. "I think she would be cool with that, because all she could talk about in the limo was how happy she is that my big brother was here to keep me in line."

"That's good to know. But I think we going to have to keep each other out of trouble. I won't pull the big brother card on you just yet, but we got to get together in a few days and do some catching up."

After promising to get up with each other, the brothers went to rescue China from the girls. When they got there, Mrs. Williams came over to snap pictures of them all together. She then introduced Asad to her curious family members who had only heard of the son but never saw him.

Chapter 31

A week later Asad and China came home from closing a deal on a building for China to open her own elder care center. They were met at the door by Bobby happily barking and wagging his tail like he always did when Asad was around.

"Sky! Sky! Why is my mother's puppy here?" Asad asked as they made their way to the bedroom where Sky was in bed watching a Lifetime movie.

"Mama asked us to keep him for her because Fred was taking her down south to meet his folks in the morning," she answered.

"Why you still in bed? You still not feeling good?" he asked as he leaned over and picked up the dog to pet him.

"We're pregnant!" she blurted out while showing her big smile.

Sky did not know how else to tell them, but her only fear was China being mad at her. They had become very close, and she loved her as much as she loved Asad.

"What? How do you know?" he asked her, before looking at her and then over to China's shocked face.

"I stopped at the store on my way home from picking up Bobby. Tasha told me the best test to get, so I bought a few of them. I took two of them, and they both say I'm pregnant," she nervously explained, looking her friend right in her eyes and trying to read her mind.

Asad dropped Bobby and just stood there with his head down. He was trying to process the new predicament he was in with Sky and China. He did not know what to say or how to feel. The only thing on his mind was hurting China.

"China, are you mad at me?" Sky asked her.

"Do you have any more tests?" she asked with a slight smile on her lips.

"What? You don't believe me?"

"No, it's not that. I believe you. It's just that my friend hasn't been around either. Just come with me," China said as she pulled Sky out of bed and into the bathroom.

"Hey, I want to come too."

"Noooo!" the women said in unison. "This is girl's time, and me and her got to talk!" Sky told Asad before closing the door on him.

Asad sat nervously on the bed playing with his mother's dog and flipping through the channels. The few minutes that passed seemed like hours. He soon heard screams of excitement, so he rushed to the door, but it was locked.

"What did it say? Let me in!"

They opened the door and handed him the two test strips.

"Here you go, daddy!" they said, laughing with joy as they hugged one another.

Asad was happy with the thought of fatherhood and relieved that he did not have to choose between the two halves of his heart.

"All I got to say is when my mother gets back, y'all are telling her this. I'm going to be hiding someplace far, far away from her!" he joked, before joining the two women on the hugs and kisses.

Epilogue

Byrd got word from one of his goons that a guy who went by the name of Von was going around bragging about murdering Zay. Byrd put the best man he knew on the mission to avenge Zay by killing Von.

"Say, big homie, this one's on me! You sure this was one of Asad's guys he offered, right?" the hit man asked with delight in his eyes.

He scared Byrd, but he would not let him know it.

"Sure as I know my name. Say, if you not going to take nothing for that nigga, take this to send a message that we ain't to be fucked with!" Byrd told him, pushing some cash into his hands.

"Okay, I ain't going to keep turning down no cash. I got baby shit to buy and hair and nails to pay for, just like you niggas. I'm still doing this nigga for free, so this covers the example you want. You'll know when it's done."

Byrd shook hands with the hit man and then they parted ways. He then gave Asad a call to tell him what was going on.

"I ain't here!" he answered jokingly.

"Then how you on the line now, crazy-ass boy!" Byrd laughed with him. "I'm glad you in a good mood. What's good?"

"Shit! Just fucking with my lil' sisters on the phone. What's up with you? I know you ain't just calling to jack with me. What's up?"

"I need you to ride down on me, or I can come by you, whatever. I got some real shit to tell you that I'm sure you want to hear right the fuck now, my nig," Byrd told him while honking his horn at a pretty face in a dark-green Corvette next to him.

When the woman looked over at him, Byrd motioned for her to pull over. She declined, raising her hand and showing off her wedding ring before pulling ahead of his truck.

"Okay, where you at now? I'm just coming from Speed Queen," Asad said, stopping his car in the parking lot's exit as he waited for directions.

"Shit, you right down the way. Meet me at Checker's. I'll be there in a few. I'm coming up North Avenue right now."

Asad made it to the restaurant first, but he did not have to wait long before his friend's big Range Rover pulled in next to him. They both exited their rides, and the two hustlers stood between the vehicles in the employee parking lot of the drive-through.

"One of my niggas gave me word about this fool named Von—or some shit like that. Do you know a muthafucka by that name?"

"Not that I can think of. What up with him though?"

"The punk's running 'round jacking about offing Zay. Rest in peace to bitches and shit."

This was not what Asad expected to hear from Byrd when he told him they needed to meet up. The thought of avenging Zay made his blood boil and his trigger finger spasm a bit.

"Where this nigga at? I got whatever you want. Just take me to this bitch," he quickly snapped.

"He runs with that cat Eshy and them Chi-town muthafuckas over on 30th and Michigan. But I got you on this already. Don't worry about getting your hands dirty. That's what we got money for. I got the best killa I know on that shit right now," Byrd told him as he re-lit his kush-filled blunt.

"That's a good look. I'm going to do a little something for you anyway and tell your man to come see me when he's done too. I got something extra for him too. This on GP, because that's some real shit you niggas did for me."

"I'll let him know. But I'm good. Zay was part of the fam, so I feel your pain too. You feel me?"

They shook hands and parted ways. Asad then went back the way he came. He got on the phone with Jasso and told him what he was told by Byrd as he drove home. Byrd got in line at the drive-through to get himself a bite to eat since he was right there anyway.

~ ~ ~

Over on 30th, Fame was breaking into Eshy's dope house basement window. He could not believe he was given this hit. He knew it would show his brother that he had real love for him and that they were greater together. Fame quickly fell inside the window. The basement was dark, wet, and filled with junk. He walked up the stairs and put his ear to the door to listen for any movement before making another move. When he did not hear anything, he eased open the door, being careful not to make noise.

Fame crept through the grimy and dimly lit house. There were dope heads passed out in almost every corner of the house. Some of them had needles hanging out of their arms and legs or wherever else they could inject the drug into their bodies. This was good for Fame, because none of them paid him any mind as he moved past them. He came up on one of the workers sitting with his back toward him. The worker was deep into a game he was playing on his cell phone. Fame quickly slit the man's throat with the knife he used to break in the window. He picked up the gun from the table, and then looked into the dead man's face to see if he had gotten lucky. But he was not the person who he had come for, so he continued moving about the shadows through the house.

Fame soon came to another set of stairs just off the dining room that led up to the second floor. He climbed them two at a time with his back to the wall swiftly but carefully. The hallway on the second floor was also dark, so he kept close to the wall for his own good. A door just behind him opened, and Von emerged from the room still adjusting his belt after using the bathroom.

As soon as Von saw Fame's unfamiliar face, he went for his gun, knowing that none of the junkies were allowed on the second floor of the house, which they referred to as the shooting range.

"Hey, what the fuck are you doing up here?"

Fame already had the gun he had taken from the table in his hand.

"I was looking for you," he answered, shooting first and hitting Von in his upper chest.

The hot slug turned Von around like a spin toy. Fame sent more shots through his back and side before Von hit the dirty floor. The blood-thirsty goon then stood over the dying man and emptied the rest of the clip into his head.

All the gunfire brought the rest of the house workers out. MJ was getting some head from one of the pretty dope women when he heard the shots over the loud music in the room he was in. He roughly pushed the woman out of his way, pulling his Dickies up as he grabbed his gun and ran from the room to see what was going on.

MJ found himself being a witness to the savage murder of one of his best friends at the hands of the stone-faced killer. Without saying a word, they quickly started exchanging fire. Fame had to dive from the bathroom's doorway to the stairs so he would not be trapped by MJ's gunshots. MJ ran after him, which caused Fame to slip and fall over the banister. The dirty couch broke his fall, but he did not waste time counting his blessings. Fame rolled to his feet just in time to dodge the shots that ripped through what was left of the pillows on the couch.

Another one of MJ's young goons rushed to aid his boss, only to be killed before he could ever prove his worth as Fame made his way out the front door. There was a scared man standing just outside of the door that Fame shot down, just in case he found the heart to use the gun in his hand. A junkie tried to grab him as he ran past him, but Fame easily slipped out of his grasp. Now outside of the house, Fame ran as fast as he could trying to make it to one of the two stolen cars that he had placed at opposite ends of the block for his getaway.

He made it just in time to witness the first of many cop cars hitting the block. They were obviously responding to a 911 call made by neighbors once they heard shots fired.

~ ~ ~

"It's done but not over. There's a lesson still to be taught that you paid for, and it will be given. Just keep watching for it," Fame told Byrd over the phone as he laughed to himself at what he just went through.

"Okay! Go chill out for the night. My nigga wants to meet you to thank you himself. He good people."

"I know. I'll get up with him in a minute, but right now I'm gone."

With that, he ended the call.

Fame thought of how Von had just lost his life trying to impress a female.

"Who says money is the root of all evil? Pussy is a cold bitch," he laughed, and then sang along with MJ as the radio played his hit song "Reckless."

The End.

Text Good2Go at 31996 to receive new release updates via text message.

To order books, please fill out the order form below:
To order films please go to www.good2gofilms.com

Name: __ _____
Address:_____
City:_____ State:_____ Zip Code:_____
Phone:_____
Email:_____
Method of Payment: Check   VISA   MASTERCARD
Credit Card#:_ _____
Name as it appears on card:_____
Signature:_____

Item Name	Price	Qty	Amount
48 Hours to Die – Silk White	$14.99		
A Hustler's Dream - Ernest Morris	$14.99		
A Hustler's Dream 2 - Ernest Morris	$14.99		
A Thug's Devotion – J. L. Rose and J. M. McMillon	$14.99		
Black Reign – Ernest Morris	$14.99		
Bloody Mayhem Down South – Trayvon Jackson	$14.99		
Bloody Mayhem Down South 2 – Trayvon Jackson	$14.99		
Business Is Business – Silk White	$14.99		
Business Is Business 2 – Silk White	$14.99		
Business Is Business 3 – Silk White	$14.99		
Childhood Sweethearts – Jacob Spears	$14.99		
Childhood Sweethearts 2 – Jacob Spears	$14.99		
Childhood Sweethearts 3 - Jacob Spears	$14.99		
Childhood Sweethearts 4 - Jacob Spears	$14.99		
Connected To The Plug – Dwan Marquis Williams	$14.99		
Connected To The Plug 2 – Dwan Marquis Williams	$14.99		
Connected To The Plug 3 – Dwan Williams	$14.99		
Deadly Reunion – Ernest Morris	$14.99		
Dream's Life – Assa Raymond Baker	$14.99		
Flipping Numbers – Ernest Morris	$14.99		
Flipping Numbers 2 – Ernest Morris	$14.99		
He Loves Me, He Loves You Not - Mychea	$14.99		
He Loves Me, He Loves You Not 2 - Mychea	$14.99		
He Loves Me, He Loves You Not 3 - Mychea	$14.99		
He Loves Me, He Loves You Not 4 – Mychea	$14.99		
He Loves Me, He Loves You Not 5 – Mychea	$14.99		
Lord of My Land – Jay Morrison	$14.99		

Lost and Turned Out – Ernest Morris	$14.99		
Married To Da Streets – Silk White	$14.99		
M.E.R.C. - Make Every Rep Count Health and Fitness	$14.99		
Money Make Me Cum – Ernest Morris	$14.99		
My Besties – Asia Hill	$14.99		
My Besties 2 – Asia Hill	$14.99		
My Besties 3 – Asia Hill	$14.99		
My Besties 4 – Asia Hill	$14.99		
My Boyfriend's Wife - Mychea	$14.99		
My Boyfriend's Wife 2 – Mychea	$14.99		
My Brothers Envy – J. L. Rose	$14.99		
My Brothers Envy 2 – J. L. Rose	$14.99		
Naughty Housewives – Ernest Morris	$14.99		
Naughty Housewives 2 – Ernest Morris	$14.99		
Naughty Housewives 3 – Ernest Morris	$14.99		
Naughty Housewives 4 – Ernest Morris	$14.99		
Never Be The Same – Silk White	$14.99		
Shades of Revenge – Assa Raymond Baker	$14.99		
Slumped – Jason Brent	$14.99		
Someone's Gonna Get It – Mychea	$14.99		
Stranded – Silk White	$14.99		
Supreme & Justice – Ernest Morris	$14.99		
Supreme & Justice 2 – Ernest Morris	$14.99		
Supreme & Justice 3 – Ernest Morris	$14.99		
Tears of a Hustler - Silk White	$14.99		
Tears of a Hustler 2 - Silk White	$14.99		
Tears of a Hustler 3 - Silk White	$14.99		
Tears of a Hustler 4- Silk White	$14.99		
Tears of a Hustler 5 – Silk White	$14.99		
Tears of a Hustler 6 – Silk White	$14.99		
The Panty Ripper - Reality Way	$14.99		
The Panty Ripper 3 – Reality Way	$14.99		
The Solution – Jay Morrison	$14.99		

The Teflon Queen – Silk White	$14.99		
The Teflon Queen 2 – Silk White	$14.99		
The Teflon Queen 3 – Silk White	$14.99		
The Teflon Queen 4 – Silk White	$14.99		
The Teflon Queen 5 – Silk White	$14.99		
The Teflon Queen 6 - Silk White	$14.99		
The Vacation – Silk White	$14.99		
Tied To A Boss - J.L. Rose	$14.99		
Tied To A Boss 2 - J.L. Rose	$14.99		
Tied To A Boss 3 - J.L. Rose	$14.99		
Tied To A Boss 4 - J.L. Rose	$14.99		
Tied To A Boss 5 - J.L. Rose	$14.99		
Time Is Money - Silk White	$14.99		
Tomorrow's Not Promised – Robert Torres	$14.99		
Tomorrow's Not Promised 2 – Robert Torres	$14.99		
Two Mask One Heart – Jacob Spears and Trayvon Jackson	$14.99		
Two Mask One Heart 2 – Jacob Spears and Trayvon Jackson	$14.99		
Two Mask One Heart 3 – Jacob Spears and Trayvon Jackson	$14.99		
Wrong Place Wrong Time – Silk White	$14.99		
Young Goonz – Reality Way	$14.99		
Subtotal:			
Tax:			
Shipping (Free) U.S. Media Mail:			
Total:			

Make Checks Payable To:
Good2Go Publishing
7311 W Glass Lane,
Laveen, AZ 85339

CPSIA information can be obtained
at www.ICGtesting.com
Printed in the USA
LVHW05s1555270718
585151LV00009B/362/P